Goodbye, Philip Roth

Goodbye, Philip Roth

MARTIN SMITH

Pleasure Boat Studio: A Literary Press
New York

Goodbye, Philip Roth

ISBN 978-1-929355-54-9
Library of Congress Control Number: 2011909513

Design by Susan Ramundo
Cover by Laura Tolkow
Author's photo by A. & R. Krongard

Pleasure Boat Studio is a proud subscriber to the Green Press Initiative. This program encourages the use of 100% post-consumer recycled paper with environmentally friendly inks for all printing projects in an effort to reduce the book industry's economic and social impact. With the cooperation of our printing company, we are pleased to offer this book as a Green Press book.

Pleasure Boat Studio books are available through the following:
SPD (Small Press Distribution) Tel. 800-869-7553, Fax 510-524-0852
Partners/West Tel. 425-227-8486, Fax 425-204-2448
Baker & Taylor Tel. 800-775-1100, Fax 800-775-7480
Ingram Tel. 615-793-5000, Fax 615-287-5429
Amazon.com and **bn.com**

and through
PLEASURE BOAT STUDIO: A LITERARY PRESS
www.pleasureboatstudio.com
201 West 89th Street
New York, NY 10024

Contact **Jack Estes**
Fax: 888-810-5308
Email: *pleasboat@nyc.rr.com*

for cynthia, my toughest reader,
and louis phillips, whose readings helped get me here

and a special thanks to jack estes, my publisher,
for making it happen

Meaning is derived from a relationship
of story, storyteller, and listener, but by
far the hardest task is that of the listener.

—Stuart Kaminsky, ***Lieberman's Folly***

PORTNOY

BY THE TIME YOU READ THIS, IF THERE IS ANYONE OUT THERE reading this, Philip Roth will probably have written twenty more novels, while I no doubt will be searching for answers to the same old questions without recognition or reward. My main purpose in putting the following down on paper—more selfish than not, I must admit—is to relieve myself of this Sisyphus-like burden I have thus far endured in Promethean silence by sharing it with you.

What's driven me to the brink of madness is this strange power Roth has had over me the past few years, although we've never really met. Now don't get me wrong. I'm not accusing him of plagiarism or any other literary blasphemy; nor am I saying that he has stuck poisoned needles into a stuffed doll of my image, or conjured up the symptoms of writer's block for me in a bubbling witch's cauldron of his own design. Nothing that obvious. But like a disease that's infested the spirit and reduced it to despair, he's either taken up residence in my brain or parked alongside the curb of my eyebrow so he can eavesdrop on my every thought. I wouldn't call it mind control yet, although it's definitely heading in that direction.

At first I considered dealing with my dilemma by turning it into fiction, which would have begun:

> You can't imagine how easy it is to buy a gun in New York. Of course, I didn't exactly amble up to the proprietor and tell him I was going to use it to kill Philip Roth. The fact is, I've never owned a gun before, or any other weapon, for that matter.

A novel (or 'entertainment,' to use Graham Greene's self-demeaning term) would have been more fun for me than any other form of written communication and may have contained more truth as well—fiction often does—but in the end I abandoned the idea because I realized that if I presented this to you as fiction I would lose any chance at credibility.

The second possibility was to pen a direct plea to Roth, asking him, in effect, why he was doing this to me and what it would take to get him to stop. But did I really expect an answer when he hadn't offered me one up till now? Not on your life. A simple letter, postcard, epistolary novel, or second-person piece of imprecation to the man who has occupied my soul on condition of anonymity would have served the same purpose and achieved, I'm sure, the same result; while there wasn't a chance in hell that Roth would join me in a Camp-David-Accord-like peace conference at a neutral site.

The third, of course, and most logical, it seems to me, was to take my growing list of grievances to you in the hope that Roth would not be able to interfere, as he has done in the past, and that there would be at least one among you willing to hear me out. If he would have stuck to the simple use of family names and quasi-personal innuendoes in his books, I might have let them pass as a form of game playing between author and reader, but when it extended beyond the pages of his fiction and entered the portals of my life, my very sanity was challenged.

I'm still trying to figure out how this symbiosis got started in the first place. Probably with my reading of ***Portnoy's Complaint***, when I, a secret devotee of the muse of masturbation, discovered in Roth not only a kindred spirit in manipulating his wee pen under the bed sheets, but one who dared, in the outlandish pages of his yellow-jacketed best seller, to sing its praises to anyone who would listen. Not that I found the work altogether satisfying. In fact, I was much more moved by the the first half of the book and experienced the Israel-based ending as a huge letdown. But in spite of my overt declarations, I was soon imitating its borscht-like rhythms as if they were my own.

My need for another quick fix brought me salivating to Roth's three earlier works, expecting more of the same iconoclastic sermonizing, the same delicious cadences I had experienced in ***Portnoy***. In a sense, he became the older brother I had been deprived of by my parents, and because he could express himself with such consummate skill about so many of the issues that haunted me day and night, I admired him even more. After all, wasn't he, by proxy, writing about my determined efforts to please my parents and failing miserably, as well as openly expressing all those masturbatory thoughts I had been too ashamed to acknowledge to friend and foe alike.

My second novel—written under the influence of another Roth, the more obscure Henry—had just been turned down with the same old regrets by some of the top editors in town. A luminary at Knopf declared that 'the first thirty pages are perfect,' but found the same perfection lacking in the remaining chapters. Another at Viking said, 'There are moments in this book I'll never forget,' and then, seeing it as a 'long story rather than a short novel,' forgot to publish it. Now it sits forlornly in my closet like a heavy winter coat on a humid July afternoon, while I contemplate slipping a couple of cyanide tablets into Roth's glass of iced tea.

In a binder alongside it is my first novel, ***The Tragedy of Felix***, which had gone through eight excruciating revisions before I realized that I was never going to get it just right, and entered it, as is, in the Houghton-Mifflin Fellowship Award contest. It turned out to be the same year Roth won with his first work, the highly acclaimed ***Goodbye, Columbus***; and he may have even then (although I doubt it) seen me as his competition. I managed not to read his book at the time, but when I finally did, it sounded so alien to me that I couldn't believe it had been written by the same person who wrote ***Portnoy***. Not only did I fail to identify with Roth's tepid hero despite the admitted similarities between us (race, religion, age, and the pursuit of awkwardness), but I found him singularly offensive (perhaps in the same way I found myself offensive), while the other stories in the prized collection were reminiscent of the all-too-familiar *au currant* Bellow-Malamud school of Jewish letters—strong on dialect and overwhelmed by weeping willow emotions—that had enslaved us from early adolescence on and were then dominating the New York scene.

Neither ***When She Was Good*** (***Marjorie Morningstar*** becomes ***Annie Oakley***) nor ***Letting Go*** (***The Adventures of Augie March*** meets ***A New Life***) added anything meaningful to my La Mancha-like first impression. I even managed to dismiss Roth's use of Libby, my mother's name, for his protagonist in the latter. Whatever I had responded to in his work clearly came into being with ***Portnoy***, not before; and, thankfully, failed to turn me into one of those goo-goo-eyed groupies ready to drool and dribble at anything that happened to leak out of Roth's prolific pen.

In another lifetime he might have been my mentor, my guide, despite our similar ages and backgrounds (I'm thinking more Jewish than Jersey), but from that moment on (although I didn't know it at the time), we became halves of a very schizophrenic twosome that has reduced me to the status of ghost writer (his title) and raised him to the heights of literary stardom. I mean, have any of you ever heard of me before picking up this book? Well, have you? Of course not! I've barely heard of myself, although at one time or another I've been mistaken for Martin Cruz Smith, William Jay Smith, Something Smith and the Redheads, the village smithy, and Oliver Goldsmith.

My one published work, ***Flora's Dream***, not my best by any means, has been relegated to my closet along with a dozen remaindered clones, and I can't seem to provide them with any worthy companions. Every time I come up with a new idea for a book, Roth ends up writing it. We meet (unannounced) in the strangest of places. His name is uttered under the most cryptic of circumstances, while mine (or the names of those near and dear to me) appears in the most conspicuous pages of his books. In short, I have become his long-lost Corsican brother. Stab him, and I bleed. Stab me, and he uses my blood to write another novel.

Nevertheless, from a chronological standpoint things progressed rather innocently between us at first despite an unflattering review (one of the few reviews I received) of ***Flora's Dream*** in the ***Philadelphia Inquirer***, its bold headline a mixed reference to my mimicry of Roth:

> **Bernard's Complaint Deserves a Listener**
> As though by accident, Martin Smith stumbles into profundity and significance in a first novel that is otherwise occupied in maudlin and self-possessed ramblings. For the most part, Smith writes like a neophyte Philip Roth, using his considerable verbal ability to eke out self-conscious, self-indulgent jests that fizz like stale seltzer.[1]

For one thing, it's hard to believe that Roth would have traveled to Philadelphia to peruse this review that has me stumbling 'into profundity and significance,' mind you, rather than getting there on my own two feet. If he did, though, two points of comparison might have provoked his ire: (1) that 'Smith makes fun of Haymisch's [my protagonist's] father in the manner of Roth's treatment of his parents;' and (2) 'that Haymisch muses about her

---

[1]Lipsius, Frank. 'Bernard's Complaint Deserves a Listener,' in ***Philadelphia Inquirer***, 2-18-73.

[his aunt] in a way that evokes all of her heritage at a deeper level than Haymisch's or even Alexander Portnoy's,' and that 'the novel approaches the older generation, which ***Portnoy's Complaint*** treats more like a punching bag.'[2]

A second review, paper and date unknown, draws an even closer parallel between the two works by calling my 'non-novel'

> [a] long lament which is equally divided between this young man's (or rather half a man's) memories of his favorite 'fairy godmother' aunt Flora Menschel in the form of a sentimental Kaddish ('And your soul, where does it fly') and his own Portnoysian complaints ('I awaken, empty-bodied, my penis melting into limp mirage of shriveled worm on cold sperm puddle.')

If that's what this Roth payback is all about, revenge for having dared to tamper with his hallowed ***Portnoy***, that at least makes sense to me. That I can understand. In fact, I understood it at the time, although I still blame my editor, Hal Scharlatt, who may have been Roth's editor at Random House (another cryptic link between us) for assuming that a book about an old lady (the one I wanted to write) would not be in demand, and encouraging me to write about a man in his twenties (probably a facsimile of myself, or a poor man's Portnoy) overburdened with complaints, a subject that turned out to be no longer in demand.

It didn't stop there, though; was, in fact, only the beginning of what has developed into a one-sided road show, with Roth tossing verbal darts at my fragile psyche. Not that my next work, ***The Freudian Hours***, about a man's evolving therapy sessions, was

---

[2]Ibid.

more of the same bottled Roth—far from it; but the book I had always wanted to write, and would have eventually written, given the time and encouragement, was a novel about the wonderful world of sports, and the special meaning it always held for me when I was growing up (a Dodger fan in the Bronx); so, of course, that was the next book Roth decided to write, under the modest title of ***The Great American Novel.***

I accepted that as mere coincidence—nothing more, nothing less—just a case of two young and aspiring writers on the same creative wave length. But when he—spitefully? maliciously?—began his book with a play on the ***Moby Dick***-opening salutation, 'Call me Ishmael,' and then, instead of Ishmael or any random appellation, came up with 'Smitty, ' the nickname I went by during my ball-playing days in Van Cortlandt Park, as the name of his wordy narrator, I had to at least question his motives.

Was he perched at his desk like a diabolical robot programmed by forces beyond my control to eavesdrop on my hidden talents, either to get back at me for something I had done—the Philadelphia review hardly seemed grounds for revenge—or to taunt me for something I was about to do? I mean, what I wanted to know more than anything was how he managed to tune into my thoughts before I could even write them down, and how he had become aware of my existence without my knowledge.

If I believed in god, felt tormented by guilt, or trusted in reincarnation, I might have considered this so-called coincidence the incipient stages of a cosmic plot to make a mockery of my literary ambitions. But we weren't exactly talking about any haunted house kind of *delirium tremens* here, were we? This couldn't have been an out-of-body experience, could it? I wasn't in need of a quasi-magical exorcist to save me from myself, was I? In desperation, I clung to the deep breath I had been taught to take on such frustrating occasions and considered the limited options at my disposal. After all, I didn't want to be thought of as a classic paranoid personality stuck in the Freudian regurgitation of his own worst fears while looking for someone successful to blame them on. Did I?

All right, so let's say he didn't have any ulterior motive and just happened to write the book that I had been on the verge of writing for as long as I can remember, and then added a parting affront by giving his writer-protagonist my name in one of those Nabokovian coincidences that neither logic nor linguistics can explain. Which brings us to the book itself, the book I should have written about baseball, given my love of the game, my backhanded Gil Hodges scoops at first base and lunging Jackie Robinson line drives to the opposite field, along with my ambition to one day replace Red Barber as Dodger announcer.

As for the writing, was it mythical, as advertised? Hardly. Epic in scope? Unlikely. Melvillian, as imitated? Not even remotely, and definitely not a work I would have wanted to call my own. Whatever appeal Roth had held for me in ***Portnoy*** was gone. Or had I merely stuffed myself on a menu of sour grapes despite a plethora of reviews and awards to the contrary? Nevertheless, there was a great sense of relief in recognizing that my early onset alter ego and I were heading in opposite directions.

If, however, the reference to me in his opening was Roth's first attempt to take control of my creative powers by fitting me into the pages of one of his books, it clearly wasn't going to be his last; although Roth's next two offerings, with their opportunistic (or so it seemed to me) pop-cultural, pseudo-sexual, quasi-political implications, mercifully contained no intimations of Smitty or Smith or my personal environs. Maybe, I dared to hope, he no longer saw me as a threat; so, seemingly free of Roth at last, I shrugged my creative shoulders and went about the business of trying to find my own voice.

All that was made to seem rather trivial a few weeks later when Hal Scharlatt, the editor I was telling you about, who had just rejected my latest novel, ***The Freudian Hours***, with deepest regrets, died suddenly of a heart attack while playing tennis on a rooftop court in midtown Manhattan. Hal had a lot of friends in the publishing world, and most of them crowded into the well-known west side chapel, probably the same one Saul Bellow had used as a model for the climactic scene in ***Seize the Day***, with Tommy Wilhelm, his pathetic anti-hero, sobbing uncontrollably over the coffin's unknown occupant.

No overly emotional outbursts interrupted the proceedings this time despite the suddenness of Hal's death. It was a solemn and tearful ceremony, made even more so by the recent birth of his son. Instead of the old ladies and gents who usually frequented these tragic occasions to mourn one of their own, most of those gathered around me were in their thirties and forties (about my age), leading me to contemplate my own mortality as well as theirs.

In keeping with my accustomed inclination for anonymity, I found an obscure spot at the rear of the funeral parlor not far from the door, among some of the standing-room-only mourners, and listened to the rabbi drone on in his hopelessly inadequate words about life and death and how one gives meaning to the other. Hal's wife, in a traditional black suit and wide-brimmed black hat with lowered veil, was seated in the front row beside Hal's three children from a previous marriage and his mother and father, whom I had met briefly one day at his home. They were mesmerized (as was I) by the procession of close friends and relatives who stepped up to the dais and eulogized their fallen hero with words that were sometimes too whimsical, sometimes too personal to be shared with the public; but I soon found myself enveloped by their grief as well as my own, and wondered what I would have said if called upon for a last goodbye.

I'm not sure what first made me take notice of the person standing next to me. There was no random sign exchanged between us, no word or gesture that I can recall. Perhaps a lull in the proceedings caused my eyes to wander. All I know is that I just happened to look up—somewhat reluctantly, I might add—and discovered that I was pressed up against none other than the ubiquitous Philip Roth. Quite amazing, wouldn't you say? But only, as it turns out, an early and harmless instance of what was to become a series of bizarre interactions between us over the years that has me on the verge of believing in some sinister Pynchonesque plot being directed against me from persons and paranoias unknown.

I contemplated saying something hopefully profound and brilliantly engaging to him, but being shy by nature, I all-too-readily refrained from opening my mouth. During the rest of the service, my attention was equally divided between the ritual leave taking being orchestrated from the dais and the impressive figure standing mournfully beside me. He looked more or less like he had in the obligatory photos on the dust jackets of his latest books. A bit thinner perhaps, his hair grayer and receding with increased rapidity, as he neared his fortieth birthday (still a year ahead of me).

My need to avoid him (both physically and mentally) intensified after this impromptu meeting. I swore not to attend any more funerals, especially those involving literary personages, and I avoided anything written by Roth except for a cursory glimpse through ***My Life as a Man*** (1974), his next novel, to make sure it contained no passing references to me.

When he began by dedicating the book to one of the editors who had turned me down twice, and then opened the first part with two stories, the main character of which bore the name Nathan, my father's name, I said to mysefl, 'Uh-oh, here we go again.' But as if he had suddenly tired of the game playing between us—or so I wanted to believe—he shirted the spotlight in part two to Peter

Tarnopol, the so-called author of the stories, and another Roth substitute, and devoted the rest of the book to dealing with some of his more solipsistic hang-ups, which no longer (at least overtly) echoed mine. Yet despite my momentary relief, the powers that be (real or imagined) had already arranged for our next encounter, which was to take place shortly thereafter in Central Park.

To get from the east side, where I lived, to the west side, where I taught two mornings a week, and back, I preferred to stroll through the park and experience the seasons first hand rather than endure the confines of a crowded cross-town bus or its exhaust fumes along the 86th Street transverse. It was during one of those solitary gambits, while lost in daydream or desultory thought, that I almost bumped into the suddenly omnipresent figure of Philip Roth, perhaps taking a break from the writing of his most recent book. He was walking toward me on a winding sand path between unoccupied ball fields, casually attired in beige slacks and an open-collared white shirt, unnoticed by the few passersby who were on their way to work or walking their dogs.

He didn't acknowledge me, and I didn't acknowledge him. We were strangers, ultimately strangers, in the park. Yet he came equipped with a confidence that I hadn't even been close to attaining in my lifetime. His movements were self-assured, nonchalant, carefree. He had no deadlines to meet, was a writer-in-residence (his own residence), while I raced from school to home in the hope of getting an hour or two in at the typewriter before the bell sounded for the beginning of my next class.

Again I considered speaking to him, letting him know that I was a writer, too, the fellow mourner who had stood beside him at Hal's funeral, but I instantly talked myself out of it as an infringement on his privacy. If I had one of his books with me, I probably would have asked him to sign it for my pet orangutan, but being empty-handed, I continued on past him, without a sign of recognition from either of us, and, quite frankly, should have been able to bury this harmless episode under the lawn of my subconscious.

That was my intention, I'm sure, and I believe I would have succeeded were it not for another coincidental meeting ('passing' might be more accurate) somewhere on the same path the following week, with both of us wearing similar attire and achieving the same inconsequential result, as if we were engaged in a ritual *déjà vu*. Because these random encounters had transported us beyond the covers of his books, they were beginning to disturb me. But they ended just as suddenly as they had begun. Although I continued to be on the lookout for him the next few weeks, there were no repeat performances, and the two of us were never to meet again.

In seeking to accomplish that end, I have gone so far as to change schools, move to distant cities, alter my reading habits. Yet despite our diverging roads—his bordered by the fruits of success, mine heading toward the weeds of literary failure—our lives came dangerously close to touching once again in another minor-key coincidence that had to leave me wondering if I would ever escape his incursions into my life.

I was teaching a creative-writing course at Finch College at the time. Although it had become known as a finishing school for spoiled little rich girls, I took the job mainly for convenience (it was located only a few blocks from where I lived) and not to discover a rich wife to support my writing habit. Despite the school's sullied reputation, I found its students as adept and committed as any I had ever taught.

The most memorable of my academic seraglio's precocious darlings were gaunt, inky-haired Michelle, as mute and moody as Poe, who wrote pastel fairy tales in Hockney-esque settings; darling Mack, with the soft blue eyes and an innocent smile to match despite her longshoreman's name and Hammett style, and with whom I might have been in love all frustrating semester, but didn't know it for sure until she had a classmate of hers hand me a farewell note after she had graduated; Nordic Susan, with her Medea-like blonde hair, dark chocolate eyes, and Ibsenesque vignettes; and Natasha, daughter of an émigré Russian princess, about to marry a Romanov or a member of the Politburo and forsake her samovar poems forever. In a sense they were mine—not sexually, of course—although I toyed with the idea on more than one occasion — but as real flowers in my imaginary garden.

Their sweet siren voices allowed me the luxury of ignoring, if not dismissing altogether, my latest fears of being brainwashed by Roth's most recent successes, despite both ***The Ghost Writer*** and ***Zuckerman Unbound*** bringing back as an encore Nathan Zuckerman, a fictional Roth clone who just happened to have the first name of my father and the last name of the nasal-toned rabbi who had tutored me for my bar mitzvah.

To add insult to innuendo, Roth entitled the successful ***Portnoy***-like novel within the novel ***Carnovsky***, the name of my favorite actor of all time (the indelible Morris), whom I had once seen riding on the subway with the peel of an orange he was eating lodged in his cuff, and later watched give one of the great performances as Lear in Stratford, Connecticut, not far from where Roth was now living. In keeping with my high spirits at the time, however, I refused to let myself be depressed by these latest examples of Roth's ability to travel up and down the landmarks of my life in his books without permission, until he had the nerve to violate my physical space as well.

Finch, being close to Central Park, had a countrified air despite its city location, and as I walked the fourteen blocks to school and back the three days I taught there, I felt like the curator of an outdoor museum. It was during one of those mornings, while arriving at the quaint turn-of-the-century architectural remnant, that I overheard two of my students at the entrance, with the buxom Susan 'dying to tell' the wraith-like Michelle of her latest sexual conquest.

'You'll never guess who I went out with last night,' she gushed, no doubt aware that a handful of her classmates and I were close enough to comprise an impromptu audience.

'Then I guess you'd better tell me,' was Michelle's ho-hum response in a voice half-bored with envy.

'Philip Roth, the writer,' she announced, as if we didn't know who he was or what he did for a living and required her editorial comment to enlighten us.

Needless to say, I felt instantly and totally violated by him again, but even more so on this occasion, for now he had invaded the outskirts of my reality, emerging from the world of fiction to seduce one of my lovelies without pause or provocation. Obviously, there was a challenge being issued here, a message being sent not through the usual channels (his words in the pages of a book), but spoken by a member of one of my classes; his way of letting me know that nothing of mine (not even my students) was safe from whatever power he possessed over me.

Without waiting for Michelle's anticipated retort, I continued on to my classroom as if I hadn't heard a word they said. But I read Susan's subsequent stories with renewed interest, hoping that she might reveal in them some tidbit about her latest escapades with Roth. She came to class looking more voluptuous than ever, but kept the hovering author to herself despite my voyeuristic longings.

Before the dust of that episode had settled, although surely not because of it, my stay at Finch came to an abrupt end. In fact, the entire school was forced to shut down due to a lack of funds or because there was no longer a need for that kind of girl's-only school in the equal opportunity world we now inhabited. In the meantime I had turned a friend's three-page treatment into a screenplay about a hardboiled detective and, based on that effort, was summoned to Hollywood to co-author a comedy about *The Wizard of Oz*. It seemed like the perfect escape from my skirmishes with Roth and my inability to follow up my first published novel with a worthy successor.

My partner (as well as best friend at the time) and I began working day and night like a couple of sit-com collaborators or how we believed sit-com collaborators were supposed to behave, with him puffing on a meerschaum pipe and me manning the old Smith Corona whenever we came up with a witty line, sitting across from each other at the round Formica table which was to become for us (for me anyway) a metaphor for the best of Hollywood. During our breaks, I ran along the Pacific Palisades as if running could rid me of my ghosts (or ghost writers).

It was not until my return to New York and the familiar pattern of seasons, after one produced (albeit poorly reviewed) film and four or five dead-end development deals, that Roth reentered my life with a vengeance. Oh, not in any preordained meeting in the park this time, the 'I see you, you don't see me' sort of game playing we had indulged in earlier, but in the blurb of his latest book, ***The Anatomy Lesson***, which I chanced to peruse over the shoulder of a bearded fan in a neighborhood bookstore.

It turned out to be the third in a series of novels featuring Nathan Zuckerman, the character with the combined names of my rabbi and dad, a strange mutation that I had chosen to let slide the first fewtimes he tried it, but now had to conclude, given the persistence of these questionable happenstances, that Roth wasn't done prodding me; for there in the blurb of the book (and again later in the text itself, as if telling me once wasn't enough to call my attention to it), among the list of lovelies who were expected to serve as nurse companions for the sickly Zuckerman né Roth during the upcoming pages, he just happened to include a Finch College coed, her name changed, no doubt, to protect the author.

Now, I ask you, why else would he have chosen Finch, and even mentioned it by name—not any college, mind you, but the one with the bird's simple appellation that also served as natural habitat for a more exotic kind of bird—rather than some harmless fictional institution of higher learning, if he didn't have me in mind? I mean, here he was, not only confirming in print what my student had alleged, but gloating about it as well, and all for my benefit, for who else but I would have noticed or cared? No Smitty, Libby, or Nathan name-calling this time, but a blatant reference to the very school where I once held court.

Roth goes on (as Zuckerman) to present his delicious conquest as being on the tall and thin side, with not much of an ass, undersized breasts, and short dark hair that seemed to convey a Louise Brooks or Prince Valiant look. In fact, the overall description of the lines, circles, soft angles, and curves of her face and body created the impression of an *art nouveau* poster girl, at least to my discerning eye, and although she was by no means bad looking, according to Roth, except maybe when sullen or discontented, he didn't exactly bestow the beauty label on her either. The word portrait might have referred to any one of a dozen Finch coeds, although it didn't sound at all like the dimpled Susan with the Kim Novak face and Marilyn Monroe figure who had boasted to the Garbo-esque Michelle about dating Roth. In fact, the description more closely resembled the enigmatic Michelle, with her quasi-mystical airs and spidery model's body, unless he had somehow seduced them all in a communal rite of spring or some sort of quasi-religious bacchanal.

In self-defense, I decided to read the Roth works I had bypassed earlier. Maybe it was at this time, in the nonfiction piece ***Reading Myself and Others***, that I discovered a reference to his use of my mother's name as one of the primary characters in his second book. I have always been reluctant to write about how I should be read—as Roth has seemingly done here—or to compose synopses for lethargic editors to shortcut through my books before rejecting them, since I believe they should speak for themselves. At first

I found nothing that pertained to me until I reached the chapter on ***The Great American Novel***, in which Roth attempts to explain away Smitty as someone seeking to turn fiction into reality (his evaluation of my work?), while the book's final chapters (under the auspices of Roth, I assume) seek to turn reality (the un-American activities of the House Un-American Activities Committee) into fiction, with me (not him) being called to the witness stand.

Let it be noted that our views of his book are very different. He sees it as a sharp detour from the literary road he had been traveling on, while for me it's more of the same old Roth taking up residence in a new domain—the world of sports. The comedy of his earlier works, according to him—whether politically corrective, as in ***Our Gang***, or psychologically revealing, as in ***Portnoy***—were limited by their ends; whereas ***The Great American Novel*** is comedy for its own benefit or enhancement, in the same mode, I suppose, as the art for art's sake proponents opted for an art with no strings attached, not only setting it free, but, according to Roth, going so far as to withdraw the comic from his comedy.

The so-called freedom that he (not I) believes he has attained here seems somewhat lost, however, in this determined effort of his to define that freedom within strict literary bounds. Yet it also allows Roth—peripherally, of course—to bring Smitty, his parody of a writer (more pointedly, this writer) back for an encore, with himself as the designated ghost and yours truly along for the ride as concerned, if not contented, reader.

And he does it well, posing at times as Roth interviewing Roth, in what might be considered his first overt display of doubling. On the surface, of course, he's talking about the book. Everything with Roth is about higher surfaces and lower depths, how much in each book is about Portnoy, Zuckerman, Kepesh, Tarnopol, et al., and how much is about Roth himself. But he'd have us believe that ***The Great American Novel*** is different, that there is only blithe, good-natured comedy involved here, nothing undermining, and that 'Smitty' is just a chance name that popped into his head one nondescript weekday afternoon; a premise that I, as son of Libby and Nathan, two of his more distinguished characters, strongly refute.

While denying that there is any sadism contained in these pages, he does reluctantly admit to its inclusion in the creation of such comedy—thank heaven for that!—since on the same page he reveals how squeamish he is about calling his comedy 'satire,' given its association with using harsh measures to achieve noble ends. Leading me to wonder if it's the noble ends that disturb him, because it sure as hell doesn't seem to be the harsh measures at his disposal. And believe me, this is no victimless crime we're talking about here. I should know, for I am the butt of its humor, the target of its destructiveness, the frontier town of its lawlessness.

In his defense, Roth tries to sell himself as being carefree rather than cruel, and downright jocular instead of jeopardizing, maybe even naughty at times, but no more harmful in writing this book than a child frolicking in a garden of verses. Yet he's doing it at my expense, let me remind you, with a series of euphemisms to suit his own purposes, under the guise of punishment fitting crime, in sentences filled with subtle asides and subordinate clauses.

Toward the end of the chapter, after an extended review of the sixties and its 360-degree reversal of values, Roth refocuses his attention on ***The Great American Novel***, and Smitty's role in telling its story, and believe me, I'm waiting with held breath to see just how he intends to accomplish his latest piece of tap dancing. But his less-than-flattering appraisal of me as being overly suspicious and a master confabulator (in response, I'm sure, to what I have been saying about him) comes as a flagrant and personal challenge to me before he goes on to reveal that his creation of Smitty has something to do (I know not what) with it no longer being possible to define America, and that, despite his best intentions, Smitty can only hope to offer up his own failure of a definition. Now let's get this straight, fellow readers: what Roth is telling us here is that this book is what America means to Smitty, not Roth. But who invented Smitty if not that master of suspicion and confabulation, Philip Roth? Smitty surely didn't invent himself, and remember, this isn't Smitty calling himself Smitty, but Smitty is being called Smitty by Roth, the self-acknowledged author of this book.

I mean, what is he basing my so-called paranoia on anyway? My more-than-justifiable concerns about him? And what makes me any more of a composer of fantasies than he? Or is he really bothered by my claims of authenticity? Remember, this is supposed to be his book we're talking about, not mine. But he doesn't stop there. As if in response to my thoughts, he goes on to explain that choosing Smitty as his spokesman allows him the perspective from which, by association, to question my credibility—in implied contrast, I assume, to the veracity of his own hallowed books—and may be a devious maneuver on his part to short circuit, even denigrate, what he anticipates I am going to write about him.

His target may, in fact, be the very work you are now reading (if anyone is out there fulfilling this writer's humble expectations). And despite his denials of being cruel and sadistic, what has to be the final rub is his ultimate ridicule of my inability to write a baseball novel by making me the so-called narrator of his.

If Roth is claiming that Smitty's fantasies are identical to those that emerged out of the catastrophes that plagued the sixties, whereas his are not, then why does he insist on incorporating so many of them in his books? Meanwhile, he implicitly accuses me of inhabiting some sort of unreal Erewohn (in contrast, I assume, to his more factual Erewhyreve), and maintains that the so-called history I am writing (with him at its center, mind you), although based on something that did take place, is totally fabricated. But isn't this history that he's made Smitty's history really his own? And how does his fiction differ from that history, dressed as it is in his usual autobiographical finery. As for mine, if it's all invented, as he claims, then he too is nothing more than a figment of my imagination, so why should he care?

In the end, though, Roth has me trying to portray in my writing the nation's seemingly incurable illness, whatever that may be; while I believe my books are more about fiction's relationship to reality, and seem not unlike Roth's efforts to find some kind of free passage between the real and unreal, while narrowing the distinctions between them. Yet his final emphasis is on what he sees as the differences rather than the similarities between us, with me trying to conjure up a legend of this country (a latent metaphor for Roth himself?), and him conjuring up a book about the creation of that legend, which has him, of course, encompassing me, and his book enveloping mine.

Yet Roth's next incursion into my psyche did not occur in one of his books, but the more volatile pages of real life, when I discovered that he and Claire Bloom had been living together for years. Hardly relevant, you might say (and I might agree), except for the simple fact that when I was in college she was the woman of my dreams. If I had read *The Professor of Desire* when it first came out, there's no way I would have missed the Claire Bloom dedication (an obvious message to me from Roth) or the Claire Bloom (fact) and Claire Ovington (fiction) connection in that book. I don't believe it would have made any difference if I had, except that I might have resented him even more, been on the alert for his sneak attacks a lot sooner, and written this complaint—Smith's, not Portnoy's—ages ago.

After all, I had to at least wonder if Roth had me in mind when he began his liaison with Ms. Bloom. Now don't believe for an instant that I'm suggesting he married her to spite me, a stance he has taken in some of his novels; but the unexpected news, the lateness of its arrival notwithstanding, catapulted me back into the fifties and my sophomore year in college, as I suspect he might have intended.

I was taking a course in Shakespeare at the time, and on occasion would dress up in my light blue double-breasted bar mitzvah suit and my only dress shirt, don my father's wide (as the Grand Concourse) navy blue tie, the gold deco tie clasp bearing his initials, and his matching Swank cuff links, paste down my stringy hair with a sticky green pomade—in one of those Clark Kent into Superman changes of identity, although in my case the process may have been reversed—and take the subway downtown to one of the old Broadway theaters in an escapist journey that instantly transported me beyond my rather mundane Bronx surroundings to the magical world of the stage.

The most memorable of these odysseys brought me, one fateful evening, to an Old Vic production of ***Romeo and Juliet*** starring John Neville and Claire Bloom, with whom I had been in love ever since I saw her play the suicidal ballet dancer in Chaplin's ***Limelight***. I arrived early, as usual, bought my ticket, received a playbill from one of the lady ushers, who looked more like waitresses (wearing white aprons over plain black dresses), and was led up the steep carpeted steps to the rarefied heights of the second balcony.

Below me, the rows of the orchestra were being filled with an array of gaudily attired remnants of the Upper East Side, while most of the seats in the mezzanine, which was separated from where I sat by nothing more than a carpeted aisle, and balcony were already occupied. I looked around for a seat closer to the stage, but by the time the lights dimmed and the curtain went up, there was none to be found.

I followed the lines, which I had learned almost by heart in class, word for word, but the moment Claire Bloom appeared on stage—with proper mother and bawdy nurse—I couldn't take my eyes off her and was barely able to concentrate on anything else. She looked more lovely and innocent than any picture of her that I had ever seen, and I vowed to love her forever.

During the ensuing intermission, I quickly glanced about for a better seat, not really expecting to find any, but noticed an unoccupied box against the wall on my right. When the lights dimmed for the beginning of the next act, I sidled over to it and hunkered down in the first of the three adjoining seats overhanging the stage. As soon as the curtain went up, Claire Bloom, Romeo's Juliet as well as my own, moved slowly forward in a virginal white nightgown, her black hair combed straight down to her shoulders, until she was standing right beneath me.

I don't recall the scene or her lines, but found myself so caught up in her spell that I leaned over the edge of the box for a closer look, when the spotlight behind me, which I hadn't noticed before and probably was the reason for the box being unoccupied, threw my shadow upon her like a threatening cloud. I'm not sure if anyone else noticed the change—I don't know how they could have missed it—but she didn't react, nor did the audience, and I instantly ducked down behind the façade of the box, where I remained hidden until the scene and the play had ended.

Although the incident involved no damsel in distress, as I might have wished, and instead of a knight bearing my name riding in on a white horse to rescue her, featured only an overly impressionable youth in a double-breasted doublet pining away for his sweet Juliet of the Sorrows from afar, with two known Romeos in attendance—one on stage and one in the audience—and one unknown (the enigmatic Roth) waiting in the wings to exchange love potions or marriage vows with her; it has stayed with me ever since, while following her career from a courtly lover's distance, until years later, without warning, Philip of Roth decides to enter her life and, in a manner of speaking, thrusts her back into mine.

What about you out there? Are you, with your holier-than-thou preconceptions about art and the misplaced artist, who may be reading this rambling confessional only because Roth's name is in the title, are you prepared to take my part in a fatal showdown in the lobby of somebody's cerebral hotel? Well, are you? How would you like it if someone named Roth were listening in to your thoughts as if they were on the radio? Is he? Has he set up some sort of mind control game with a menagerie of types like me—all writers, all aspiring, all unsuccessful; or all readers, all devotees, all eagerly awaiting his next novel—the lot of us inadvertently supplying him with witty plot lines and intricate denouements. Or am I, when all is said and done, the sole object of his disdain? Not that I would have written any of his books, but I might at least have written my own.

PATRIMONY

WHEN IT COMES TO ***PATRIMONY***, WE'RE NO LONGER TALKING about the book I would or should have written, but the one I was actually working on when his hit the stores, and that has to frighten me. Whatever has brought us to the same subject—our struggle with a parent's death—at the same time, I find it the most moving of Roth's books. Yet it also serves as a cruel reminder that mine is still unfinished.

The opening chapters offer a number of possible generic links between us. When, for instance, Roth praises his mother's cleaning prowess to the skies, he might have been speaking of my mother as well. But then again his remarks are just as applicable to about any Jewish mother worthy of the designation, and not only mine. A reminiscence of his father and his working buddies getting together for a weekly pinochle game at Roth's house conjures up visions of Morris Kantor and my aunt Faigel warring with my cigar-smoking father under the *shabbus* candles, or any card-playing family threesome, for that matter, Jew or Gentile, although the more memorable pinochle games for me were those I played with my father for hours on end almost every day while nursing him back to health after his stroke.

When, upon registering to enter the hospital, Roth's father discovers it would cost a few dollars a day to watch TV in his room, he turns it down at once, and even afterward rejects his son's offer to put up the money for it; in doing so, he is not only reenacting what my mother had done on more than one of her hospital visits, but the behavior of hordes of their parsimonious brethren. Even

Roth's decision to go for a stroll in Central Park and clear his mind after having received the crushing news about his father's condition can be seen as acknowledging our two near meetings there years ago, or just filling in a lull between dramatic sequences.

But these are all, I must admit, rather subtle points of analogy between us and probably wouldn't stand up in a court of law or public opinion. The one clear indication that Roth still has me in mind, however, is the Claire de Bloom refrain that he keeps playing over and over throughout the book as a reminder that she's still with him and therefore not with me. Claire, Claire, Claire, on pages here and there, but not necessarily anywhere significant in the book, since her shadowy presence remains in the background most of the time as a trail of well-placed asides and incidental appearances. Oh, there's a lot of the Claire returning to London, Claire being phoned, Claire making soup, Claire having coffee, Claire sitting and listening, Claire going to dinner kind of inclusion, usually as part of a Claire and me, or Claire and him, or Claire and he tandem, with Roth's father as the third person pronoun being referred to, and Roth as the more distant first.

One might, of course, argue that she was there so why shouldn't she be mentioned? And I would answer that (1) her presence hardly advances the plot, and (2) she never utters a word during all of her so-called scenes in the book. Oh, she's there all right, and Roth is anything but shy about letting me know it; at least her *name* is there. But she moves from page to page without benefit of a description or spoken word, so that only someone who is familiar with her (like me) can imagine what she looks like or sounds like or what she's doing there in the first place. I mean, why the extended silence? Didn't she have anything of note to say during those patrimonious days and nights? Or is she merely intended as a silent muse serving as a conduit between Roth and his ailing father, and now, more pointedly, between Roth and me?

Before I can get comfortable, though, Roth tosses out what seems, on the surface, no more than an attempt on his part to rationalize his reluctance to level with his father about his condition by evoking a time when his father hadn't been completely above board with him.

As reiterated by Roth, it concerns the death of his mother. He was in London at the time (*with Claire Bloom*, might be read between the lines), when a call came from his father informing him that his mother had suffered a severe coronary and he should come home at once. But when Roth called back to let him know his plans, his father started weeping and admitted to Roth that his mother had in fact died while having dinner with him earlier that evening.

If that's what happened to him, then so be it; who am I to question its validity in the scheme of things? But it comes suspiciously close to an event in my life that I was trying to put down on paper while Roth was writing ***Patrimony***, and I can't help but question his purpose in including it here.

My experience occurred during the early sixties. I was teaching a composition course at the American University, playing the part of Mr. Smith goes to Washington years before Roth began writing a book about his father dying of a brain tumor or I was even remotely aware of something called Alzheimer's disease, when the dowdy English department secretary entered my classroom one seemingly harmless afternoon with a look of concern on her pillowy face and announced a call for me in the office. Probably the last thing I expected to hear was my mother's tearful voice over the telephone telling me that my father had been taken to the hospital with a heart attack and that I should come home right away.

I cancelled my class at once, rushed to my apartment to pack a bag, and hailed a cab out to the airport, realizing on the way that I had forgotten to ask my mother what hospital my father had been taken to. During the ominous flight to New York, I kept hoping that he would still be alive when I got there.

After arriving at Newark Airport (I'm not sure whether it was the earliest flight I could get or because I was so confused while making my reservation that I didn't realize where the plane would land), I called my mother to find out the name of the hospital. Upon hearing my voice, she burst into tears. 'Where are you?' she demanded. 'What's taking you so long? Come home already! Don't you know that your father's dead?' And now years later in ***Patrimony***, not reminiscing about my father but his mother; not set in Washington, D.C., this time but London, England; not my mother on the phone but his father, Roth provides a variation of my tale of woe with his of *déjà vu*.

In following with the tefillin episode some twenty pages later, Roth shines an overhead light directly on my guilt, while perpetuating the guise of writing a eulogy for his father. It's the ongoing balance between the two that creates the ultimate tension in the book for me. To maintain that balance, Roth has his distraught father, who is obsessed with discarding many of his possessions in anticipation of his approaching demise, reveal to him how he had disposed of his tefillin, leading his disappointed son to wonder why he hadn't been the recipient of that gift.

I can't remember what, if anything, I did with my father's tefillin after his death, or whether they once belonged to his father. I was not living at home at the time and might have left the getting rid of my father's belongings to my mother. The only possession of his that I ever really wanted, despite my reluctance to wear any jewelry, was my father's pinkie ring, but my mother had a jeweler friend remove its one stone without telling me and use it to make a gaudy ring for her, then either discarded, misplaced, or lost the rest of it, probably because it had little monetary value, although it was the only part of the ring that meant anything to me since it had my father's tiny embossed initials on its face.

But the incident also raises from the dead my one encounter with my father's tefillin, which were kept in a small blue velvet bag, along with his tallis and yarmulke, in the foyer closet. After deciding at the last minute not to attend the bar mitzvah of a friend one Saturday morning, I was so overcome by guilt that I donned my father's tefillin—winding the strap of one of the small leather boxes to my forehead, the other to my left arm—for the only time in my life, as if their mystical Hebrew words would somehow absolve me of what I experienced as a sin.

The motif is picked up by Roth several pages later, when, after leaving his father's apartment and climbing into his car, he unwrapped the gift his father had given him, which turned out to be the shaving mug that had once belonged to his grandfather, and a keepsake that he had clearly let his father know he would like to have; while I, in marked contrast, gave away the utensils my blacksmith grandfather had made in Russia and my Aunt Faigel kept hidden in the bottom of her kitchen cabinet until her death. Maybe I was too young at the time to realize what they would mean to me later on. My parents weren't big on memorabilia, and since the items were rather crudely made, I decided, to my everlasting regret, that I had no room for them in my apartment. Roth's bond, though, I offer in my defense, was with his father, not his grandfather; and I'd like to believe that if my grandfather's creations had been cherished by my father, I would have wanted them as much as Roth wanted his grandfather's mug.

Barely giving the reader, especially this reader, a chance to catch his breath, Roth turns his attention to me again under the guise of making a rather cursory observation about how his father seemed to look up to, even admire, the more debonair, world-renowned doctor he went to for a second opinion in contrast to the portly, plain-looking brain surgeon he had initially consulted. It's the kind of comparison that most readers, including myself, might have passed over without the slightest pause; and I would have as well had it not been for his use of the Yiddish word *haimisher*, in its traditional sense of down to earth or unassuming, to characterize the first doctor's appearance—the very word, let me emphasize (as Roth has done by putting it in italics), upon which the name Bernard Haymisch, the protagonist of my Portnoy-inspired novel was based—with its obvious *shtick* and stones reference to my only published work.

Although Roth occasionally resorts to Yiddishisms in his myriad volumes, why here, why now, why this particular word among the rich lexicon that has become part of New York slang if not to belittle my main character and his modest creator, as well as the book itself? From what I can figure out, ***Patrimony*** seems to be revisiting the guilt-evoking events of my life as well as Roth's. I am not about to argue with him over chicken or egg privileges, though. Let his events precede mine, if need be. It's not so much which came first, but why these particular moments have been chosen from his autobiographical archives.

The next guilt trip he takes me on, and a brief one at that, is driven by his fear, not uncommon—and, in fact, shared by me—of surpassing his father. His may have occurred some time during his college years, but mine had its roots a lot earlier and in a much less conscious place. Perhaps it had something to do with my father's foreign birth and his lack of a formal education, but it manifested itself when I, an expert speller in school, kept writing 'definate' instead of 'definite' and thought little of it, until years later, when my usually reticent shrink, Freudian by nature, said to me, 'You're a Joycean scholar, what do you make of it?' Only then did I realize the 'defy Nate' significance. True or not, it was a theory I had no trouble accepting, although he never provided an explanation, Joycean or other, for why I wrote 'reccomendation' instead of 'recommendation.'

Roth also creates a stark contrast between his factual father and one of his repertoire of fictional fathers. The father of Nathan Zuckerman, for instance—that mixed name once again that brings me back into the mix—hated his son's negative perception of Jews in his works, while Roth's father was infuriated by the critics who considered his books as loathing both Jews and self. My mother, as I judge her, clearly comes down on the side of the fictional father. In empathizing with my critics, she no doubt saw herself (probably with some justification) as one of the Jews being attacked by me rather than the hypocrites among them.

One reviewer—Ribalow, Rahv, or Rumpelstilskin (I'm not sure which, or if it was in fact any one of them)—Jewish by name as well as affiliation—in the last of the only three reviews I received for ***Flora's Dream***—attacked me in the same way Roth was attacked, for shamefully showing Jews in a bad light in my work; although I continue to maintain (to critics and readers alike) that all I did was turn on the light, not tell them how to behave there, and what I wrote wasn't about Jews *per se*, but about people who just happened to be Jewish and therefore the people I knew best, having grown up among them.

The other attack, personal and frontal in nature, came from a distant family member, a rotund, bespectacled rabbi about my age (and related to me by marriage), whom I had always known as Cousin Seymour (someone the family, both his and mine, spoke of with much reverence over the years), although I had never met him before. It was at a wedding or bar mitzvah he had just presided over that he confronted me. I'm not sure if he introduced himself or was introduced to me. Before I had a chance to say anything, he asked me, with a solemn look on his face, why I had to paint the Jews with such a dark brush when there were enough anti-Semites around to do the job. Taken by surprise (I was expecting a congratulations for having been published or a 'welcome, nice to meet you' salutation), I had no retort handy, nor did I feel it proper to take on this so-called religious savant among us, who had come at me without warning, bearing the family colors (my mother's among them) on his sleeve, in some heated verbal exchange whether on synagogue or ballroom floor.

The last word, as it always must, came from a reader. It is the only letter I ever received from a reader, and it made me wonder if Roth had received many of the same or only letters of acclaim. It arrived unexpectedly in a small manila envelope. On the front, under my name (which is neatly written in blue ink), the Dutton address is crossed out with three lines of red ink, and mine, inserted below (also in red ink). On the bottom left of the envelope are written the words, "Author *Flora's Dream*," clearly identifying me. Pasted almost directly in the center of the back of the envelope is a stamp (not postage) that shows a snake with thick black, white, and orange stripes crawling along on dry desert sand past the bones of a creature or creatures long dead. On the bottom right of the stamp, in capital letters, are the words SONORA KINGSNAKE. The letter itself is torn along the bottom as if something has been cut out, folded in half, and then in thirds. It reads as follows:

> Dear Mr. Smith:
>
> I am amazed to think that Dutton—or any decent publishing firm—would put out such filth as your book: "Flora's Dream." I should have read the first few pages before taking it home for reading over the Memorial Day weekend, but unfortunately read only the jacket cover at the library and was misled into thinking it had a respectable moral. However, less than two pages of obscenity were enough. And to dedicate it to your parents!

> You are evidently trying to follow in the footsteps of that bum Philip Roth—exploiting the Jewish race by misrepresentation, really—and it would be a small loss to them—and humanity in general—if you drop dead before you become a more "promising" author. Why not sewer digging to which you are better suited?
>
> An Ardent Admirer
>
> P.S. And to think that you taught classes to deaf children in Washington, D.C.

It is but another curious link in the chain that binds Roth and me into a single package, although I don't feel I can attribute this one to Roth's doing—can I?—since he seems to be as much a target of the letter writer's venom as I.

But nothing glues us together from head to foot as much as the scene in which Roth goes in search of his father, who has been gone from the table where they had been dining much too long, and finds him standing naked (after having attempted to shower) in a bathroom covered with shit. Maybe it's a more universal situation than I have ever realized, and many of you out there, like me, can identify with Roth, down on his hands and knees, cleaning the feces-bespattered bathroom until it was spotless again.

The most memorable of my mother's shitting fiascos occurred the day before my wife and I had decided to move into a smaller apartment in our building to lower our rent. I was sitting at my desk when my mother called out from her bedroom in what I had come to recognize as her organic or ***Exorcist*** voice. It was a low, throaty demand more than appeal, a craggy remnant of some sea monster's tortured bellow that would summon me or my wife to help her get to the bathroom.

I'm not sure where my wife was at the time, but I hurried to my mother's room at once, helped her out of bed, grasped her awkwardly by the arm, and tried to lead her to the toilet.

Her movements were rigid, spastic, carried out in robotic cadence. She kept pleading with me not to rush her, that she couldn't go any faster, although there was nothing physically wrong with her. As we moved forward in slow motion, the shit began escaping from beneath her diaper and landing in an archipelago of droppings on the floor.

Once I had finished cleaning up after her, although not even remotely matching Roth's Herculean effort, my wife and I decided that moving into an apartment with one bathroom was out of the question, but that didn't prevent me from enduring several repeat performances of my mother's beshittings, which tended to trivialize each of them compared with the one grand epiphany involving Roth's pathetic father that would provide a moving scene for his son's book.

Let me assure you, Felipe de Rothko, that I commiserate with the shame you may have felt for your father's outcast state, and I strongly identify with your dire sense of pathos, but it wasn't half so awful, it seems to me, as having to lower my naked mother's now flabby body into the tub for one of her baths, or lift her out when she was done, in violation of every Oedipal taboo since primordial times; while my wife, who wasn't strong enough to do the ignoble deed herself, supervised from behind. Seeing the awful embarrassment on my mother's face, which must have mirrored the embarrassment on mine, I managed to utter in feeble self-defense, 'You did it for me once, Ma. This is my chance to pay you back.'

And now, with my mother no longer among us, I am at last unburdened of the fear that I would be forced at some point to send her to a nursing home, which I swore never to do. 'One day,' she said to six- or seven-year-old me while riding on a bus or trolley past a home for the aged on Kingsbridge Road in the Bronx, 'that's where they're going to put me when I'm too old to take care of myself.'

'No, Mama,' I protested. 'I won't let them.' But who were the 'they' and 'them' we were talking about? Was it not I, the grammatically correct guilty party of the paragraph to be? And was this not a warning, a threat, a Cassandra-like prognostication destined to fall on deaf ears? And who the hell was I ever to believe that I could prevent it from happening?

We grow up, we grow down, we leave home, we become our own adults, we make parental-like decisions about our parents, we grow old and die, but we continue to play the children's games we once played at home. Our wives are our mothers, as we are their fathers. We dance the same dance at their feet as they danced at ours, but I refuse to or cannot put it down on paper, while Roth turns the terrible burden of dealing with his father's tumor into an award-winning book.

In doing so, he tackles a number of father-son issues, all of which pertain directly to me. When, for instance, he defends himself against those who demean the significance of being overly devoted to a parent who has lost his ability to fend for himself and is close to the end of his days by maintaining he was as devoted and caring when his father was a lot younger and in good health, I'm sure he's bringing it up here because he is quite aware of how I cared for my father after his stroke, and that in some ways I grew closer to and more fond of my mother during her Alzheimer's days, when so many of her defenses had disappeared, allowing me, I'd like to believe, to let go of mine. And maybe what he's trying to point out is that when my parents had their health and their faculties, I was not as thoroughly in their corner as I should have been, or as he was.

In articulating his youthful wishes for a wiser, more cultured, and more worldly figure to replace the father whose lack of schooling caused him a certain degree of embarrassment, Roth again expresses sentiments that come close to echoing my own (along with guilt accompaniment) when, in high school, I brought my writings to my friend's erudite, well-read, ex-lawyer mother for her approval and, at least on one occasion, provoked my mother to tears for not having shown my work to her.

The most troubling part of the book for me occurs when Roth abruptly ends his father's convalescence from his biopsy at his Darien home with the rather casual announcement that the latter was prepared to go back to New Jersey, making it seem like it was the old man's decision to leave and not his own. What made him so prepared? I'd like to know. Was his body healed, his spirit restored, his brain no longer tumored? In truth, he seems more discarded than set free.

To Roth as well? Or did he close his eyes to the obvious signs? Apparently not, since he notes his father's sudden depression at week's end and wonders if the rage his father was manifesting on the return trip home might be meant for him. Wonders? Only wonders? Not realizes or comprehends or discerns? The anger that Roth clearly senses and his father overtly manifests doesn't seem that camouflaged to me. In fact, in order to free himself from its impact, Roth feels the need to rationalize it as his father's inability to come to terms with his own mortality. To me, though, it had nothing to do with metaphysics, but with being forced into exile by his own son.

Despite my initial outrage, I am not sitting here in judgment of Roth, but trying to determine whether I am expected to empathize with his shortcomings in order to recognize my own. Although I had brought my mother to live with us, there were times when, instead of keeping her company in front of our building, I would selfishly rush off in search of first editions in the neighborhood thrift shops while leaving her alone for precious minutes that I now wish I had back again.

If I said something that inadvertently hurt her, she would retreat to her room and threaten to leave. 'You and Cyndia [her name for my wife] played a trick on me, and now you have everything and I have nothing. I want to go away from here. I want you to put me in a home.' 'Fine,' I'd lash back. 'If you want to go into a home, we'll put you in a home,' and I'd stomp out of her room full of sound and fury despite her dementia, still caught up in our eternal mother-son struggle over money, with me hating her for being so cheap, and then hating myself for being so much like her. Later that evening or the next morning, in tears, she would ask me to, 'Please forgive me, Martele. I didn't know what I was saying,' making me feel ten times worse than before.

In retrospect, I'd like to know, how did Roth balance reality and memory? Did he run upstairs to his room after each of these episodes with his father and write it all down in shorthand, or did he record it on tape while the event was actually taking place? I once prided myself on being too involved to step outside of these life situations with my mother as Roth has done with his father, and behave like the writer I am supposed to be, but I'm not sure anymore, since he has succeeded on two fronts, as both son and writer, while I have triumphed at neither, although a book would have surely helped even the score.

Roth's goal, simply expressed, is to be as precise and thorough as he can possibly be, to omit absolutely nothing in recalling and retelling the story of his father so he can leave a lasting memorial to him, which he has surely done in this book. His words are a variation of an answer I once gave years ago, 'To keep my family alive,' to the question, 'Why do you write?' Yet despite my best intentions and a handful of unpublished books, my mother finds no such Messiah in me, while Roth raises his Lazarus-like dad from the dead at every reading.

Much of what he presents in ***Patrimony*** can be viewed as strictly father-son business mixed in with a fair amount of show business. But I am there all right, whether he chooses to admit it or not. As we near the finish line, and with it, hopefully, the end of my own unfinished symphony, I come upon a scene that can only, on the surface, be called self-indulgent and must cause one to wonder why Roth would include it in a book about his dying father. Is it meant to trivialize life as well as its end by measuring the deaths of millions against the dying of one? you might ask. Or is it supposed to represent the reduction of death in its most heinous expression (the Holocaust) to the ridiculous (sex as pornography), and literature's helplessness in explaining either one of them?

In it, Roth's father asks him to help get his friend's book published, which he believes is about the Holocaust but turns out to be a highly graphic exposé of his friend's sexual prowess during Hitler's Germany. Maybe the episode can be interpreted as having theater-of-the-absurd connotations, interweaving sex and death in a grotesque black humor requiem parodying many of Roth's earlier works, and suggesting, as the friend's manuscript does, that things are not always what they seem to be; more specifically that ***Patrimony***, albeit couched in the obsequies of metaphor, is not about a dying father after all (as I have been saying from the very beginning), but its devoted reader.

Despite many signs to the contrary, the focal point of this rather brief, albeit ludicrous interlude is not a dumb Holocaust book or its dumber concentration camp author. Nor is it death, mass murder, sex, or literature; but, more specifically, Aaron Asher, the editor Roth's father would like to have publish his friend's book, and the final rubbing of salt in my literary wounds. For of all the editors in all the publishing houses that sit in judgment of all the random books that have been submitted for publication in the world, it is the same Aaron Asher who, after having read ***Flowers***

for the Dead, my second book, sat across his desk from me and proclaimed, 'There are moments in this book I'll never forget,' and 'There is nothing you have to learn about writing,' his words lifting me in euphoric orbit high above my chair; then brought me hurtling back down to earth again with the devastating proviso, 'but I've decided not to publish it because I see it as a long story rather than a short novel.'

I left his office crushed, uttering to myself the rhetorical question, *If the person that loves you isn't going to marry you, who will?* Since then I have held the belief, fairly or not, that things would have turned out differently for me (maybe I would have become Philip Roth) if he had only published that book, but there is no way of knowing for sure; and, outside of myself, who really cares? Yet like a rejected suitor I brought my next book to him as well, either because I trusted his opinion (which I'd like to believe) or because there's a lot of the masochist in me. He called ***The Freudian Hours*** 'an ambitious undertaking,' but turned it down with the caveat that he wouldn't have published ***Finnegan's Wake*** if it were submitted to him today. Only then did I realize that, try as I might, he was never going to publish any work of mine in this lifetime.

And now, without warning, Roth resurrects him under the guise of a bit player in what may well be a black humor tribute to Primo Levi and a farewell to part of himself, very much like the Claire Bloom refrain, not once, not twice, but with eight specific mentions, mostly in the form of questions being asked by Roth's father about whether Aaron Asher, Aaron, Asher, Aaron Asher might publish his friend's book. Oh, it's all fun and games, of course—as if the name repetition were a form of brain washing, and mine, the brain being washed—until the truth of the mystery book is at last revealed. For me, however, the *coup de grace* comes with Roth's story about his father submitting another friend's book to Asher several years earlier, its being published, and Asher's taking father and son out to lunch; while I, of course, as in the untold but implied afterward, received only a rejection for my efforts and ate alone.

As I approach the closing pages, I realize that Roth has been saving the best for last. But first he tries to soften me up with the rather startling news that all his major arteries had become almost completely clogged, and he needed a quintuple bypass. At about the same time, believe it or not, on the other side of town, I was forced to stop short in the street one morning on my way to school, unable to breathe or take another step until several minutes had passed and I could move forward again without any chest pain. The following week, discovering that two of my arteries were more than seventy percent clogged, I found myself in the hospital for an angioplasty. Of course, whatever game is being played here—Simon Says, Follow the Leader, or Can You Top This?—Roth defeats me once again five arteries to two, as one would expect, and bypass over angioplasty for degree of difficulty.

The scene shifts back to his father, now unconscious, with Roth, sitting at his bedside, telling him in a whisper that he wasn't going to be able to keep him alive. As for myself, I had no such choice, since my mother was already dead when my wife and I arrived home from a weekend in the country, but as Roth describes his moving deathbed scene with his father, I am reminded of the time my mother, with glasses and false teeth removed, already looking like a concentration camp victim, was placed on a stretcher, about to be operated on for a blood clot in her leg. I truly believed that I was saying goodbye to her for the last time, albeit without any personal message to whisper in her ear a la Roth since we weren't alone and I didn't want her to hear the despair in my voice or see the tears in my eyes. Only when the surgeon emerged from the operating room several hours later to reassure me that the operation had been a success, was I able to breathe again.

In the end, what we have here is the death of a father paralleling the death of a mother, nothing more basic than that. Yet Roth comes out of the ordeal with a book, while I emerge with pages of regret. What would have been my ***Matrimony*** started out as a novel telling the story of my parents' birthplace in Russia and the writing of its memorial book, with my mother even helping me by translating passages from the original (another way of remembering her). I just couldn't, I told myself, take advantage of her childlike state while she was alive (as I believe Roth may have done with his father) by turning it into a puppet show for the eavesdropping world to gawk at.

I also feared that it would distance me from her (as objective writer rather than only son). Yet now, looking backward, I can't help but marvel at how hypocritical I have been since I knew I was going to write about her and the extent of her Alzheimer's disease after her death. I mean, was it any less ghoulish of me, despite my pathetic rationalizations, to have described her funeral in a book before she had even died?

Believe me, I am not trying to be holier than Roth. In fact, I am angrier with myself for not having been able to write about a dying parent than with Roth's viewing of his father's demise under a magnifying glass. He may explain himself best when, in analyzing a dream he had of his father, dressed in a winding sheet, blaming his son for having buried him in inappropriate clothing, Roth sees it as a symbol of his having written ***Patrimony*** with his father on the verge of dying.

Whatever his ultimate purpose in revealing this dream of an outmoded family rite, it brings together two indelible incidents in my life. The first was a dream I had several weeks after my father's death, or at least logic tells me it was a dream, although at the time it occurred (and even now), I felt as if I had awakened in the middle of the night and, looking out the bedroom window of my D.C. apartment, saw what I believed was my father mailing a letter at the corner. I dressed quickly and hurried outside to greet him, but, to my utter dismay, found no one there. The second has to do with my forgetting to 'dress' my mother in her hearing aid, eyeglasses, and false teeth before her burial, and not having thought about them once until her coffin was being lowered into the earth, although I hardly need Roth to remind me.

Her hearing aid, shaped like a miniature heart, is still on my desk in the same yellow plastic container where she kept it during the night for fear it would fall out of her ear while she slept. She kept maintaining that she didn't need one, but when we left the doctor's office with it planted firmly in her ear, her eyes widened at the street sounds she hadn't heard in years. Beside them are her thick glasses. Hanging from their wiry arms is the loose cord that held them in place about her head and now dangles meaninglessly against her grinning false teeth.

This odd trio looks, listens to, and leers at me as I near the end of this tireless tirade, for that's all it amounts to anyway. The Roth monkey has not been removed from my back, but continues to ride me as if I were its own personal rickshaw. Having reached the end of this desperate call to arms, I am not fully satisfied with where it has taken me, and I don't just mean back to the beginning. Detective fiction, in its formulaic denouement, would no doubt have provided an explanation free of charge and a gift-wrapped culprit to go along with it. I have no such *deus ex machina* resolution, although you may, if you wish, consider Roth the culprit, and my mystification the conclusion.

So what do I do now? Go through the motions of trying to get this manuscript published, or send a copy directly to Roth for his amusement? Nothing much seems to have changed. Oh, I may be a bit lighter on my feet by a couple of thousand words. There may be some cathartic value in having gotten it out of my system and down on paper, although that desired release has thus far eluded me.

Look at it this way: You become a hitchhiker, get picked up by a man in a panama hat, or by a fancy novel in a yellow jacket, and there's no telling where you might wind up.

Maybe in Panama City, Panama, or Newark, New Jersey, for a look at the lighter side of life. Drive your own car, and you may find yourself taking the same route, only this time the destination is a street in the Bronx, with a corner candy store as landmark.

What did I expect to happen anyway? A man takes possession of your identity. How can you prove it's still yours? He takes that identity for a ride, mob style, or on a tourist trip to places that you have only read about as a child. Who are you kidding? And do you really care anymore?

For those of you who have been on this ride with me from the very beginning, I'd like to thank you for having shared this intimate view of my ongoing struggle with Roth. I wish I could have given you a more satisfying resolution to what I've had to endure over the years rather than one of those 'Where do we go from here?' endings that have dominated post-modernist fiction of late.

As for the effects of ***Patrimony***, it leaves me no wiser nor more vindicated than I felt after having read any Roth book that included me in its pages. In fact, I feel as if I've been left at the side of the road like a bad hit and run. My only hope is that in seeing me lying there along the way to wherever you are going, you may have paused a moment and listened to my endless rambling with an open mind.

But whether you believe me or not (and I hope you do) or you accuse me of paranoia (and some of you will), I'm through trying to convince you. You can just go on dreaming your Flora's dreams—beauty, after all, is in the eye of the reader—until it's time for the big sleep or the long goodbye or the farewell to arms or the last of the Mohicans or the end of the road, but by then it will be much too late for either of us—you as reader or me as writer—to do anything about it.

SHYLOCK

DON'T BE ALARMED, DEAR READER; THIS IS NEITHER AN ENCORE nor repeat performance, but a return to the scene of the crime to alert you of Roth's latest attempt—in *Operation Shylock*—to undermine my efforts to place the truth about us before you. I don't even have to read a word of it to know what he has in mind. The mere discovery that this so-called confession of his deals with the theme of doubles warns me (and through me, I hope, you) of the chicanery a desperate author will resort to when feeling threatened.

Right from the opening sentence I feel that I am battling the book and not Roth. There is something final and all encompassing about it. Although I know it's not the last book that Roth will ever write, I sense that whatever has been going on between us will somehow be resolved within these pages. Maybe the title, which sounds like a military exercise and can be read as a subtle warning, has something to do with it. The word 'operation,' aside from evoking the verbal surgery Roth has performed on me in his books, suggests Eliot's etherized patient in 'Prufrock,' which of course rhymes with Shylock, a name that evokes Sherlock, England's most famous detective, as well as Venice's infamous Jewish merchant and a person under the lock and key of an inhibiting personality.

I mean, here I am feeling free again for the first time in years after having completed my own confessional—call it catharsis, call it an awakening, call it sleep—concerning my strange involvement with Roth, whether that of alter and ego or other less-celebrated pairings; when he circumvents my efforts to communicate with you through a seemingly innocuous book about *doppelgangers*, dualities, displaced persons, and the like, featuring Roth and his supposedly obnoxious double, in which he has done unto him in fiction what he has been doing unto me in fact, and making it seem that I've merely borrowed his idea. What *chutzpah*!

Not that I'm totally surprised by his tactics. In fact, at just about every moment during the writing of this manuscript I have half-expected Roth, pen drawn, to step out of the dark alley of his words with a well-orchestrated response to my accusations. After all, how do you escape the omniscient? With a quietus? A bare bodkin? The melting of your 'too too solid flesh' into puddles of despair?

His decision to treat the doubles motif throughout instead of his usual name dropping—my mother's name here, my father's name there, the name of a place I may have visited, a shocking call from Smitty to pull me out of my lethargy—suggests a more direct approach between us. He doesn't even wait for the opening chapter, but begins the preface, first paragraph, with an odd disclaimer, in which he cavalierly declares that he has had to modify some of the facts in his book, not to protect the innocent, mind you, but due to some so-called mysterious matters of law.

So before he even states the facts, he negates them, leaving the reader (you, me) in need of some clarification. Because once you are forced to deal with alterations of any kind, no matter how minor, and have the word 'number' used as an approximation in place of a specific number, there is no telling where you may end up, or whether you'll end up anywhere at all. On the basis of Roth's verbal mumbo-jumbo, therefore, one has no choice but to question the book's authenticity from beginning to end. I mean, how much can you trust anyone who is inhibited by forces beyond his control, no matter how minimal he claims the effect of those forces to be?

To add to the growing confusion, Roth begins his supposed 'confession' by telling us that he found out about his so-called double in January [my birth month, let me inform those of you who refuse to see what's going on here, the 5th to be exact], 1988, although the year, other than its being my 50th, draws a blank. He then goes on to characterize his double as some kind of lunatic—perhaps to plant the idea of insanity (mine?) in the reader's (your?) mind.

Well, let me begin by saying, I refuse to accept the premise that the thoughts of this *mashuginer* Roth has created out of his own mad desires are mine or have anything to do with me, especially his crazy idea that all the Jews should be removed from Israel before they are destroyed and returned to their pre-Hitler homes—where anti-Semitism grew like weeds in the *goyishe* gardens of Europe, and Jews were never truly a part of any country they inhabited despite their desires—so that the cycle of wandering and persecution can begin all over again. Like you didn't do a good enough job the first time, guys, so let's take it from the top.

Until Roth actually comes face to face with his double, he isn't convinced that there is such a person. If he has me in mind, as I maintain, he's got to be kidding, since he's been haunting my creative life for years. And if he's still accusing me of being his double because I may have borrowed his voice for one book, then why doesn't he come right out and say it, and not make insinuations under the subterfuge of addressing some clown duplicate with Diaspora longings? I exist out here on my own, looking like myself (not Roth), thinking my own thoughts (not his).

But Roth gives the screw yet another gentle twist when the two men meet—one seemingly authentic, one supposedly duplicitous, both intensely fictional—by having his double embrace him, in tears, as if he had just safely negotiated the wilds of Central Park after dark—another reference, no doubt, to our near meetings there several years ago, although ours occurred in the morning. Using a night image, of course, might serve as a metaphor for the unexplained shadowy union that exists between us.

By shifting to the Demjanjuk trial, he takes a giant step in my direction. For one thing, I recall having been asked by a lawyer friend to cover it, although I have forgotten for what purpose. So another parallel, albeit minor, has been drawn up between us (although I eventually decided not to go, I don't remember why). In jogging my memory, however, I now realize that it was the Eichmann trial (same place, different time) I was being considered for, so either Roth is being diabolically subtle by linking the two separate trials, or I am trying to create parallels that do not exist, which, if true, is by no means intentional. One also has to wonder what the trial is supposed to represent, and which of us, Roth or Smith, is on trial. Probably me, since, as judge and jury, Roth obviously has the last word.

In making Israel the scene of his denouement, he returns us both to the conclusion of ***Portnoy***, and a place which, for whatever reason, I have avoided visiting my entire life despite the large number of relatives on my mother's side who have lived and died there, while Roth travels back and forth between the two countries as if he were its ambassador to the U.S. Not that I wasn't a long-distance aficionado when I was growing up, following, over the radio, the heroics of the Irgun and Stern Gang in its war of independence, and, on TV, Abba Eban's articulate defense of the beleaguered state at the U.N. Yet, in a manner of speaking, by setting his novel in Israel, Roth brings me there for the first time.

We're talking about dueling banjos here—one heard, one unheard—playing this sham of doubles in counterpoint to my book about two writers locked in a war of words. Whatever Roth's long-term goals may be, he is quick to offer a recipe for how to deal with this self-imposed double, and that is to ignore him, since his main objective is to get one's attention; with Roth representing himself as the one being put upon in this role-reversal charade he's arranged for your amusement, while trying to camouflage how I've been put upon by his double-edged words over the years.

Finally, he turns himself into a ventriloquist and speaks to me through the mouth of his dressmaker's dummy, even though I have accepted my anonymity among the earthworms of literature. It's not sympathy or recognition I seek, but for Roth to leave me out of his novels and let me write my own. I mean, what in god's name is going on here anyway? Is he bugged by my lack of success, my absence of notoriety? Does it bother him that nobody knows my name?

Meanwhile his book, which claims to be about Jews, wanders about from page to page like a wandering Jew. I, being one of them, have never felt a true sense of belonging (even in the good old USA, where I was born), and still belong to no stream or mainstream of consciousness as I wander among the myriad plot lines of this carefully maneuvered book—from Demjanjuk to Appelfeld, whom Roth is interviewing for an article, to his demented cousin to the meeting with his unsolicited double and then with his double's once-anti-Semitic girlfriend to a visit with his angry ex-college Arab amigo in Ramallah back to the trial to Double to Demjanjuk to Demjanjuk's son to deep blue sea or Red Sea to secret agent Smilesburger to the diaries of the *Andrea Doria's* Klinghoffer and back again as if there were a logic to its picaresque pattern (and perhaps there is) that includes anyone and everyone who will serve as a sounding board for Roth's eternal concerns—with his double representing his doubts about himself; Appelfeld, his Jewish sympathies; and friend George, his ongoing debate with himself about the slings and arrows of being a Jew.

Yet when all is said and done, ***Operation Shylock*** is about none of these despite the façade that's been created out of a contemporary ***Who's Who*** in the B'nai B'rith. As Roth sings another song of himself—and aren't they all?—this one with himself as first person subject, he resembles a sleight-of-hand magician trying to keep his audience distracted from this Holy Land of a novel's true focus, which just happens to be the careers of two Jewish writers—one praised, one buried, yet both with immortal longings; and ends up not so much anti-Semitic as anti-Smith.

Of course, the peripheral Claire is still at his side when the curtain goes up, this time as his wife, his way of letting me know that they're married now. Repeating her role in ***Patrimony***, at least in the beginning, as a silent partner, she hovers elusively about the page rather than on it, and on the outskirts of events rather than in their midst, more for my benefit, I'm sure, than to develop his plot; although she is finally allowed to express her heartfelt concern about the troubled and doubled Roth until he leaves for Israel, when she is summarily withdrawn from the book as an active participant.

I don't know how his quasi-breakdown, brought on by an apparently routine knee operation, fits into the equation, since I can't identify with the former and have avoided the latter despite torn cartilages in both knees. Does he actually expect me to believe that his resulting paranoia, depression, and heightened feelings of anxiety, seemingly induced by the sleeping pills he had been taking, has something to do with our ongoing hostilities? Then again, this may just be another of Roth's efforts to garner more sympathy from the reader at my expense as he had done in ***Patrimony*** with his quintuple bypass. I mean, here I am in the middle of telling you how he has practically captured my mind, and he starts to bemoan the deterioration of his; in effect, mocking my frustration at his ongoing antics toward me by usurping victim's privileges in his book.

At their first meeting, Roth's double does everything but bow down before the original, lavishing all kinds of praise on Roth's books as if they were religious icons, with special kudos for ***Letting Go*** and Libby (my mother's name, remember) Herz, one of its main characters. Yet despite my having fallen under the spell of ***Portnoy*** in my teens—and I am not, for one moment, trying to diminish the extent of its effect—I never did and still do not, like his sycophantic double, consider ***Portnoy*** one of the great novels of the fifties and sixties, my jealousy notwithstanding, although I offer no alternative for your consideration. Nor have I shown a particular preference for his books over those of other authors. In fact, excluding parts of ***Portnoy*** (which made me drool) and most of ***Patrimony*** (which almost brought me to tears), I never considered myself an aficionado of the first order.

So if Double is supposed to be a replica of me—in other words, some crazy person that believes he's Roth's double or wants to be his double or thinks he's his double or is trying his best to become his double—what he has coming out of that choreographed double's mouth is not even close to expressing my thoughts about Roth or his books. Although the clichés of aging may have muted some of our physical differences, I do not speak like Roth or write like Roth or wear his novels on my chest like a local librarian. In short, we are not doubles but a more complicated sort of tandem. Whatever he may be trying to imply, it is not Martin Smith he's writing about here but the two-for-a-nickel or buy-one-get-one-free Roth.

As if in response to my denial, Roth has his double inform him (his way, of course, of informing me), in a strange reversal of roles (character overseeing author), that he is an expert on the facts of Roth's autobiography. The statement, under cover of fiction, might have been an attempt on Roth's part to acknowledge his uncanny awareness of the intimate details of my life and unlock the mystery of how and why the two of us are so inexorably linked together, but he immediately makes light of our relationship by having his double first (tongue in cheek) proclaim the impossibility of the existence of doubles, but then playfully insert the caveat that, like it or not, these phenomena (causes without effects, effects without causes) do exist.

Somewhere during their ensuing exchange, Roth is unable to keep his feelings under wraps and begins to rant and rave at his overly obsequious double while informing him—the very creature he has created, remember—that he would like more than anything to make him disappear from his life, an obvious echo of what I have been saying about Roth ever since he started using me as a punching bag in his novels. Yet when his clownish double bursts into tears, Roth, instead of using this opportunity to add something significant to the discussion and finally enlighten me as to his motives concerning Double and myself, can only go on the defensive. Hiding behind the guise of paranoia, he experiences the tears as part of a put-on by said double intended to make fun of how helpless he (Roth) has been made to feel in his (Double's) presence. In turn, I am asking myself whether said Roth is manipulating said moment to once again mock my outrage at being under his power, when he (in response to my thoughts or Double's display of emotions?) suddenly does a complete about face and erupts in uncontrollable and unending laughter that leaves Double frozen in place and me wishing for some place on the page to hide.

In his subsequent dialogue with Appelfeld, one of several that provide a philosophical background for the book, the emphasis, interestingly enough, is on the relationship between author and reader, thereby bringing me and my book back into the picture, but from a more distant vantage point, as well as part of a more collective entity. Roth, in fact, sees the reader, especially an intelligent one, as having a significant role in Appelfeld's novels by supplying the depth and dimension that his characters are incapable of possessing, given, among other factors, their limited vantage point from which to view themselves historically.

A noble thought, it seems to me, with munificent author relinquishing some of the authority over his book to lowly reader, but whatever his intents, the so-called facts to be focused on are supplied by the omniscient author, in this case the recalcitrant Roth. As for the ingredients the reader adds to the process, do they necessarily mesh with those of the author, and in the final analysis does it really make any difference? Roth, through the seeming wisdom of Appelfeld, is being somewhat slippery here, weaving me back and forth between subject and object without allowing me the depth and dimension he so graciously promises.

Spokesman Appelfeld, in his turn, takes the baton from Roth and outlines what seems to be his blueprint for writing fiction. It entails the belief that trying to capture reality in and of itself can be extremely limiting, and although for the most part the materials he uses are autobiographical, he shapes them, structures them, sets them to words and rhythms in such a way that something new and totally different emerges.

Taking his thought to its logical conclusion and applying it to the works we have been discussing, one has to wonder if ***Patrimony*** was an attempt by Roth not only to assuage his guilt, but also to justify his behavior toward his father by editing it into submission; and if ***Shylock*** is nothing more than an effort on his part to rewrite (actually pre-write), through the masquerade of a highly distorted comedic lens, this very serious personal history of mine being submitted here for your perusal? As for myself, I have always thought of a work of literature as an island located somewhere between the writer and reader, with neither having greater access to it than the other.

When Double's messenger-mistress-moll delivers a letter from her mate to Roth, while conveying his distress at how deeply he's disturbed Roth, it may be his way of letting me know how much he has been disturbed by my presence in his life over time, or, more likely, poking fun at how disturbed I have been by his interminable hold over me. And why the hell shouldn't I be? I want to know, when Roth refuses to stop using me as a target. This time he has his double do the honors, in his letter to Roth, with the denial of being a smith (this Smith, of course, complete with lower-case put-down) when it comes to the use of words, compared with those of the mighty Roth, thus demeaning my ability as a writer once again.

Roth, however, rejects her attempts at reconciliation by declaring that his only concern is how to separate himself from his double and end the chaos that the latter has caused in his life (meaning me again, I'm sure, although I still haven't been able to figure out why or how without his assistance, and feel, despite his lavish protests, that I am the one who needs instant separation from him). But then, in another about face, he goes on to question the very existence of his double, finding him lacking in those qualities that make a person real, and morphing him into a virtual person or no person at all. And I am beginning to hope that if he believes I don't exist anymore, maybe he'll forget about me and replace me with his double or another diligent reader.

To compound the madness, though (both his and mine), and further complicate the relationship between us, he presents himself as being caught in the grasp of some tremendous power (seemingly supplied by his double) that has a lot more to do with creating the plot of this story than he does. So, if you are attempting to follow Roth's logic, as I am, in several rather brief paragraphs I have gone from being his double entendre causing mass confusion in his life to lacking the accoutrements of someone real to being the so-called power behind the story that he—Roth—has written; which makes absolutely no sense to me at all unless Roth is actually referring to my narrative, not his, and what I am in the process of saying about him.

Meanwhile he continues to present himself as closet victim and me as some kind of cleaning apparatus swallowing up his remains or his residue or his debris or whatever he chooses to call it. *Who the hell are you kidding, Roth?* I am tempted to shout down at the open page in utter frustration. *You can keep your damn dust particles, for all I care. Just stop leaving me in the dust of your vindictive novels!*

As for my own personal hygiene, I clean my carpets with an old toothbrush and comb and haven't used a vacuum in years. After all, I am not the only person to have ever borrowed a fellow-author's voice (but that was in another novel, and besides, it's out of print). I mean, haven't you also borrowed from Kafka, Henry James, and Henny Youngman (by your own admission), Lenny Bruce (by mine), as well as at least a half-dozen other Catskill comedians and their lesser-known relatives?

Wherever his myriad plot lines may eventually lead, the ongoing dialogue between Appelfeld (the voice of reason) and Roth (the voice of emotion) keeps bringing us back to the theme of doubles as displayed in a variety of literary and psychological contexts, factual and fictional circumstances, and errant, unkempt disguises. The key to their discussion and the book, however, is contained in Appelfeld's observation that Roth's double (or his mock heroic copy of me) is somehow beneath him, and demonstrates less ability at pretending to be Roth than Roth would, at pretending to be him, leading to the conclusion that Roth is going to do a revision of him.

And suddenly Roth's motives become very clear to me. It's the rewriting of my book and the dismissal of my accusations against him that ***Shylock*** is all about. I mean, he's admitting it quite openly, don't you agree, albeit as fiction instead of fact, and therefore for your entertainment rather than edification? In truth, this may be a warning, through Appelfeld, that his goal is to edit me out of existence entirely and into a facsimile of the absence of being; if not a ghost writer (his title, remember, not mine) or the ghost of a writer, then perhaps a ghost reader.

But believe me, he won't be the first to try. Jerome Charyn, at whose wedding I was best man, transformed me in ***Darlin' Bill***, his prize-winning novel, to Martin, a horse that dies of mange, and Smith, a confederate general who is banished from his homeland, thus eliminating one bird with two names. And let us not forget Ionesco's ***The Bald Soprano***, a play I taught in college, in which the two families, the Martins and Smiths, may not die in the end, but are hardly alive when the play begins. So whether Ionesco chose my name out of a Dada hat, or whether I betrayed Jerry or he betrayed me no longer matters. What does matter is that Roth is not a friend, but a nemesis, the ghostwriter of Chanakah past as I am the ghost reader of Chanakah present.

What a veritable merry-go-round! I become Roth, he becomes his double, his double becomes me, and I become he—as convoluted as any funhouse can be, but one that has to end with the magician's world-famous disappearing act. Not rabbit nor cat in hat nor lady in closet nor card up a sleeve this time, but a character in a story being written, as Roth has indicated on more than one occasion, without the detached participation of an omniscient author.

So what wish does he come up with in the face of all these mindless shenanigans? Why, what else would a narcissistic author with delusions of grandeur wish for in the climactic pages of his own book—not merely wish for, mind you, but even covet, with its ***Scarlet Letter*** connotations—but to be removed as far as possible from the spotlight and whatever innocuous character it may be innocently focused on. Meanwhile I am trying to figure out which of us, Double or Devoted Reader, he is calling for to be exiled for an extended period of time (or, to read between the lines, be done away with altogether) under the guise of desiring it for himself.

But when he compares Appelfeld's ability to remove himself from his works with his own reluctance to make himself disappear in his, are the verbs he uses to suggest this self-destruction intended as bold vocatives or harmless declaratives? More to the point, which self does he have in mind? Is he contemplating murder or suicide, and, if the former, am I the intended victim? By calling for the departure of his ego and his beaten-down self, is he trying to lure me into doing the same?

Roth admits that he has been thinking of divided selves for quite a while now, including my self, I'm sure, and how many other selves among you who might have incurred Roth's wrath? In a sense every protagonist he has ever created can be seen as his double, a theme that seems to have always obsessed him. Although he's approached the subject objectively through Anne Frank, I don't believe he's ever treated the object subjectively before, as he seems to be doing here. Yet he reverts to the Victorian novel for his definition of the double as the manifestation of a respectable person's dark side; with Roth, of course, representing himself as the respectable original, and me as his depraved copy.

Although he admits to being aware of all the available literature featuring doubles, Roth denies that he had any intention of writing on that subject. Of course he didn't, not until he found out that I was doing a book about him. Then he has the nerve to complain to you—in all seriousness, I presume, despite the comic attire he has donned for the occasion—that he was being frustrated by someone (*moi?*) seemingly unknown to him and not even remotely connected to him, which is precisely a reflection of how I feel about him. In response, he comes up with what he believes is a brilliant notion, and that is to name his double, thereby minimizing his (and by extension my) importance in his life.

Rather than use my name or nickname, as he had done in ***The Great American Novel***, which would have been too obvious for words (his, of course, not mine), he turns me into Moishe Pipik, a mock heroic name chosen out of our Jewish childhood (containing, by the way, *the same number of letters as my name*) that I must admit to having forgotten along the way to growing up. A combination of the mythical Moses with the mundane navel, it is used to disparage or diminish someone with grandiose aspirations, but without the skills to get him there; or to put a haughty someone (undoubtedly me) in his place.

The first name of this divided self might be meant to represent Roth leading the children of Israel out of bondage (according to his double's insane plan), and the second, me contemplating my own navel (or novel) in the light of his infuriating parody; with you, I assume, expected to laugh out loud at the belittling of my book as well as my name. Roth even engages in some Nabokov-like word play, in pointing out the repeated vowels with their doubles connotation (the lower case i's, no doubt, a subtle reference to his double and/or me as diminished first persons). But he does seem to have overlooked brave young Pip of Dickens' ***Great Expectations*** as well as the prophetically painful 'oy' in Moishe, which I have uttered on more than one occasion in response to Roth's unwelcome intrusions into my life.

Yet just when he seems on the verge of abandoning his purple Pipik passages and dealing with some of the relevant issues between us, Roth takes a sharp turn off the beaten path and travels along a lonely Palestinian side street (both literally and figuratively). Once there, he bumps into his Arab pal curious George, who, believing that Roth espouses the views of his double, guides him on a joyless journey during which he spews out a hate-filled history of the Jewish people leading to their moral disintegration and dehumanization, which may be Roth's way of concealing some of his own negative feelings about Jews in general and me in particular. This brief, seemingly impromptu interlude literally transports him out of his self into an otherworldly place that culminates with Roth assuming the role of his double among his Arab *compadres*.

After a number of near-harrowing experiences (whether real or imagined?), he is returned to his hotel room by an Israeli soldier who had, in another of those inevitable Roth coincidences, just finished reading ***The Ghost Writer*** and strongly identified with the father-son relationship of Nathan Zuckerman (the combination platter of my father and rabbi Roth has served up on a number of festive occasions). His double is already there, awaiting him like a dutiful member of the Jewish National Fund to collect the cool million that Smilesburger mistakenly donated to Roth. Double begins by trying to let his original know how intimately connected their lives have been over the years. The numbers and degree of involvement may be off, but the sentiment is clearly mine, although I would have demanded an explanation along with it, which Roth may not need from his double and seems unwilling to give to me.

He then playfully rubs more salt in the wounds when, feigning innocence or ignorance or both, he asks his double what he does for a living; and the latter, to my amazement (if not Roth's), lets him (and therefore me) know that he's a private eye. And I am left staring down at the page in utter disbelief, because by turning his double into a detective, Roth can only be making light of the fact that I teach a course in the detective genre, have written several articles about the form, and completed a private-eye novel (unpublished) based on a friend's three-page treatment, which he then turned into a screenplay (unproduced) that brought me out to Hollywood for a brief encounter of the third kind. When Double, in describing some of his duties, relates how important words are in his line of work, the premise is that he's talking about his career as a detective, but it might just as readily be Roth flaunting his writing accomplishments at me while belittling mine in the name of his other.

During their exchange of anecdotal pasts, Double intimates that he knows a good deal more about Roth's life than your run-of-the-mill imposter; in fact, one has to wonder out loud if he is Roth. He also tells a curious tale about guarding President Kennedy, a particular fan of ***Letting Go***, who mistakes Pipik for Roth, as a young woman at a party in D.C. mistook me for JFK, and invites him and William Styron, whom many people at McGraw-Hill felt I reminded them of when I began working there in the early sixties, to a future meal. In terms of plot, one can surely accept the incident as confirming the physical likeness between Roth and his double, but it would be hard to ignore the tie to me that Roth achieves by selecting these two particular individuals from the crowded top hat of characters at his disposal.

As is his wont, once Roth reinforces the connection between us, he has his double sing his praises as if they were coming from my mouth, bow down before his hallowed image with the reverence and adoration of a fanatical worshiper, even go so far in his reverence as to be ready, willing, and able to accept from the Roth menu of literary appetizers whatever concoction he decides to offer up. And all I can do as passive reader (along with you, if you're still there), is partake of the same cuisine with neither bang nor whimper, but a bibbed child's stoic silence.

After listening to several of Double's missing persons detective stories, Roth refers to his antics as nothing more than another of those one-man performances that can be seen on TV or heard on radio, and wonders out loud what part or parts in them the mighty Pipik is playing. In response, Double accuses him of being just like every other writer in believing that everything is a game. He even traces the source of Roth's arrested development to his having listened to that children's show on the radio that Roth identifies as 'Let's Pretend,' a program, by the way, that I also listened to as a child, devotedly if not devoutly, in one of the more benign connections between us), although its Cream of Wheat sponsor was never a particular favorite of mine despite its hauntingly familiar theme.

But when Double continues his harangue by charging Roth with being the last of the great pretenders, there's no doubt in my mind that Roth is directing his words at me and my book, which he's trying to get you to believe is pure fiction and has no basis in fact. Having, by his own admission, occupied Roth's head for an inordinate length of time, Double has finally come to the realization that all writers live in a fantasy world. And I, in turn, have to wonder, while trying to keep track of Roth's ability to speak out of two mouths (his and his double's) at the same time, if this is a semi-Freudian slip on Roth's part or if he is admitting at last, through messenger Double, what I have been trying to tell you from the very beginning of this book: that he has indeed had access to my thoughts all along.

Among his list of complaints, Double bemoans the fact that Roth avoids him, refuses to pay attention to him, and resists his attempts to reach some kind of rapport with him, which is precisely how I wish Roth would behave toward me, although I can't help but identify with his accusation that Roth steals from him, since every time I come up with an idea of late, I find it or its variation in one of Roth's books, as he exhumes from god-knows-what subliminal landscape the buried treasure of my thoughts; the latest, of course, being this doubles fiasco that he keeps doubling back on me by voicing my preoccupations as if they were his.

Double is befuddled, as I have been on more than one occasion, by Roth's insistence on seeing him as a threat. But just when I'm expecting some ultimate punch line from Roth to tie everything together in a neat Victorian package, he comes up with the anti-climactic, Dadaist, theater-of-the-absurd-like appraisal of his double and maybe the very story he is telling as having absolutely no significance whatsoever; and in a way, under the guise of giving himself advice, warns me not to waste my time looking for any.

Meanwhile Roth's double responds to what he considers a threat (from me or his famous author?) with the challenge, carefully wrapped in another double entendre, that he used to make to the more pugnacious criminals he pursued and caught to show that he had no fear of them. He'd shout out his name (Roth's, too, of course) and let them know he can be found in the book (signifying ***The Yellow Pages***, it would seem), a word which Roth repeats, then highlights with italics and an emphatic exclamation point. Well,

I'm in the book too, man, Philip Roth's book, into which he's trying to lure the part of me that isn't already there, while doing his best to discredit the part of me that is, as well as (by association) the book I am in the process of writing.

In response to this last episode of Double's autobiographical TV-like detective stories, Roth can no longer contain the volcanic eruption of laughter he feels he should have released since first becoming aware of the former's existence. Whether it's aimed directly at me or the almighty Pipik as my stand-in, he is accusing one or both of us of seeing him (Roth) as the object of our aspirations, the complement of our unfinished selves, our *cause célèbre*, the fulfillment of our promise, the person we most saw ourselves like when we weren't looking in the mirror, our ultimate spokesperson, the being for whose identity we were willing to discard our own. If, as it seems, he has left me (I can't speak for his double) without ego, without hope for success, without any faith in myself when measured against his self-proclaimed omnipotence, then why, may I ask, have I been selected as the dart board of his disdain?

To further lighten the mood, Roth comes (pun included) up with his usual sexual hi-Jinx (pun extended), as in the good old Portnoy days and masturbatory nights, whether it takes the form of verbal foreplay with his double's damsel over the telephone; or the huge erection that Pipik magically pulls out of his fly as if it were a homeless pet, but turns out to be a pathetic implant before Roth tosses him out of his room; or the house detective disguised as its number one pervert, who keeps offering blow jobs through his peephole, all of which eventually leads to the first nocturnal emission Roth has had in ages and (when combined with every other unpleasantness he believes he has endured during his stay in Israel) his on-the-spot decision to leave the Holy City as soon as he can.

Turning his paranoia inward, Roth suddenly feels that he is in imminent danger of his double for not having had taken him seriously. Utterly frightened and confused, he believes he hears Pipik speaking to him from outside his door, but then realizes its his own voice he's listening to, and that he's actually having a conversation with himself. The effect, perhaps intentional, is to make both Double and me disappear from the premises without so much as a second thought, and lead Roth, after shoving a dresser in front of the door, to question whether any of this has actually occurred.

Following his usual pattern, and perhaps as an escape, he reverts back to his familiar 'Jews are us' motif, contemplating the treatment of *goyim* in the novels of Malamud and Bellow rather than the dismantling of a Jew in his, while constructing related questions for his upcoming interview with Appelfeld. At this point I'm ready for almost anything, including Roth's emerging from his book, fists bared, ready to fight me to the death. Yet he fakes me out once again with what he presents as a goal he would like to achieve, and that, believe it or not, is to make himself vanish. And become what? I ask myself. A missing person for Detective Roth to find? Or is this his way of subliminally inserting the idea of disappearing in my head so he can have me transformed into an invisible man in place of the very real one sitting here in my pajamas writing a book about him?

Whatever the reason, he follows it up with another brilliant sleight-of-hand by telling himself not to put it down on paper at some point in the future since no one will believe any of it anyway in this age of skepticism, mistrust, and doubt. So in effect, under the guise of exploring his options, he first ridicules my fear that no one will believe what I'm saying by expressing that fear as his; and then, by telling himself not to write about it, couches what amounts to a warning to me as a harmless afterthought. Yet despite how impossible it supposedly is (for me, he must mean) to convince anyone of the validity of what I am saying on these pages, he plunges ahead in the following chapter with a supposedly 'real' visit from Pipik's lady friend to warn him that Double and Meir Kahane are planning to kidnap Demjanjuk's son and mail him back in separate pieces until his father admits to his crimes.

During their desperate exchange, she even asks Roth to take her along with him. Then, while lying on his bed and telling him her life story as Double had done before her, she awakens in him erotic longings associated with his first wife. He realizes that he'd better get out of there while he can, but makes love to her instead before heading for safety. Whether fact or fiction, the impromptu tryst brings to mind (mine, not Roth's) the lovely Claire waiting faithfully at home for his return. Roth may see Double's lady fair (or fair lady) as sexually attractive, but I definitely do not. Reubenesque women have never appealed to me. Claire Bloom is my cup of tea. Yet Roth has her with the taking of toast every morning, then makes sure I know about it by the afternoon.

To change the subject once again, and in doing so seeming to take a more objective view of what he's trying to accomplish on these pages, Roth temporarily steps outside of his narrative to inform the reader—in effect agreeing with what I have been telling you all along, although there may be more method to the madness than I am willing to admit—that his book is burdened down with too many plots for any one of them to take hold, as if he were critiquing a work that had been plotted by someone other than himself, and I don't mean the plots he's been hatching on every street corner to cover up what his book is really about, namely me.

Another possibility, of course, is that he's referring to this very work you are now reading (mine, not his), with its traditionally singular plot in contrast to his plot of many colors, while disguising himself as an impartial observer of his (not mine); or this may just be one more example of Roth circumventing my criticism—this time of his plot—with an overt display of self-flagellation. Finally, his dividing of self from fiction into fiction and fact may in fact be part of his plan to maneuver me from fact into fiction, with his ultimate goal of getting me to become him (or his double), think his thoughts (or those of his double) rather than mine (with no double to call my own), and in the end lose my identity in the ensuing maelstrom of divided selves and dead souls.

Yet rather than approach me with peace offerings and open arms, Roth becomes quite demeaning, as he questions how deep a person I am as well as my ultimate worth in the hierarchy of the universe (as compared, I'm sure, with his and his myriad accomplishments). Furthermore, under the guise of discussing the relationship, in the abstract, between author and character, he continues his lowering of my self-esteem by putting me in one of his books, under his surveillance, claiming that I am incapable of creating a coherent plot of my own (while he can create so many, whatever their direction or purpose may be) without the benefit of his expertise, and ends up (in the usual pot and kettle syndrome) by accusing me of stealing (my work as well as my life, mind you) from him, all of which I strongly deny.

In my own defense I'd like to say that I am not and have never been dependent on the writer (except, of course, for the writing he has provided me to read), as he may believe, unless I am the writer he is talking about. The reader too, for that matter. He, if anyone, is the resident thief around here, anticipating my every thought as if it were his own, which he does seem to admit when he is forced to ask himself why the writer (he, in this instance), in treating Double and/or me as closet rivals, takes from us as well. Leaving me once again to wonder if he is actually telling the world, even if only by innuendo, that he has 'borrowed' ideas from me as well as his double? Whether he is or not, he at least acknowledges it as something the writer is capable of doing and that happens to be on this particular writer's mind, meaning his this time, not mine.

In attempting to justify his odd behavior when he played the role of his double in Ramallah before an audience consisting of pal George and his Arab chums, he comes up with such feeble rationalizations (not unlike those he used when he sent his father home in ***Patrimony***) as the theoretical switching of subject and object, himself and his double, in order to better understand his creation (another way of describing what I am trying to do here with regard to Roth and his other self) or the more innocent game playing of a practical joker (like he supposedly did in ***The Great American Novel***) just having some good clean fun (at my expense, of course). Yet at the same time he seems to contradict himself by referring to his ongoing confrontation with Pipik as occurring along the meanderings of a plot that was somehow taking shape without the benefit of his input, thus once again refusing to take responsibility for his words, even in his own book. I find myself in total perplexity, wanting to ask him, who the hell else is running this perpetual road show if not you? The characters you have created out of a gaudy imagination, or your loyal and obedient readers? Roth seems to answer by raising an incongruous white flag, declaring his double the winner, himself the unconditional loser, and leaving me wondering to myself where do I go from here?

But that doesn't prevent him from continuing to toy with me as well as his double, this time by presenting himself as being on the verge of leaving Israel, his double, the book itself; and, believe it or not, I am on the verge of buying into it, when a *deus ex machina* cartoon supposedly induces him to turn around for what he claims will be a winner-take-all confrontation with Pipik. Yet despite this latest development, I can't keep my hopes from soaring. This will resolve it, I tell myself. This will bring down the curtain on our elaborate *pas de deux*. Just Roth against me. *Mano a mano*. No Pipik passes, no anti-Semitic hi-Jinx, no Appelfeld saws of wisdom, no pathetic Klinghoffer diaries or descendents of six million Holocaust victims seeking redemption or retribution at the foot of the Wailing Wall.

Clearly, we're coming to the end of the line. Roth himself pulls no punches, vows to wipe out his double (and, by proxy, me) for once and for all, calls for an old-style gunfight at the O.K. Corral (as I have been doing since before I began this book) between lawman and lawless, authentic and imitation, omniplotted and plotless, successful and discontented, adept and inept, author and reader, and whatever other polar opposite pair of doubles you may come up with in your exploratory voyages through all the thesauruses that ever existed on library shelves spanning the erudite world; with me, of course, ending up as the composite villain of the piece, and Roth as its white-horsed hero. Oh, I know he's going to win all right. After all, he's at the controls (despite his endless denials), not I, but I'm still hoping for some answers and perhaps a bit of closure before we arrive at the last page.

Fortified with a sense of outrage and a pedestrian motto calling for his double's total demolition, Roth enters the King David Hotel ready for battle, but I am up for the challenge, looking forward to it, in fact. Although he comes at me doubly armed with hero and self, I don't mind the two-against-one odds or the added voice at his disposal and whatever it may have to do with turning thought into being. Every comment he makes about his double seems to come at me with double meaning. But instead of the showdown he and I are expecting, Roth is told (and, in effect, tells me) that Double isn't there anymore, that he's departed the premises, which at first sounds like a possible death knell, maybe even mine, but turns out to be his abandonment of Israel, as Roth had intended to do.

Instead of taking no for an answer, Roth decides to one-up his double by playing the detective as the latter had played the writer—a variation of, if I (Smith) could be Roth, he (Roth) could be Smith—and goes upstairs to search Pipik's abandoned room for clues. He finds a strand of pubic hair and some fragments of a cut beard, which he puts in separate envelopes, and will eventually keep on his desk, alongside two pieces of memorabilia from his multiple adventures with his double, while writing ***Operation Shylock***. Despite its seeming innocence, as a further blending of Roth and Double, the event comes at me as another comment on my mother's paraphernalia—false teeth, glasses, and hearing aid—that are lying before me as talismans as I write this book.

When Roth acknowledges how hard it was for him to accept the idea of his double, who am I to argue, since I'm having a tough time accepting Roth's presence (double or nothing) in my life under any circumstances? On second thought, I'm not at all sure which story he's talking about, mine or his. If his, then why is he having such a hard time with it, since he's the one offering it up to the reader for acceptance? If mine, it can only serve as another attempt on Roth's part to discredit what I am writing about him.

After all, isn't this Roth's Tin Pan Alley confession we're reading here? I mean, who brought up the notion of doubles in the first place? Have I been flaunting it in his face like a victorious flag? I may be writing about Roth's perverse impact on me, but not as a double, never as a double. Maybe Donald Barthelme, whom I did not know, always waved to me in Greenwich Village because he thought I was Roth. Maybe it was part of a practical joke the two of them were playing on me for their own amusement. In any case, I always waved back politely while trying to understand his motives. Roth even goes on to question the validity of his own character, and although I agree with him, I can't help but wonder if the comment is being directed at me, especially when he questions my ability to make it in this or any other world.

Those of you who identify with Roth, admire Roth, pay homage to Roth, think of Roth as your literary guru will no doubt defend him as an innocent author being attacked by a jealous reader consumed by paranoia. I'm missing the point, you'll tell me. This is nothing but typical Roth humor. Merely a play on the doubled Dostoyevsky, the bi-Part Poe, the secret Conrad, the quilty Nabokov, the second White from the corner, the twice-told Hawthorne, the tale of two Smittys.

Then how do you explain the appearance of Libby in his second novel? The introduction of the wordy Smith in his seventh? Do you believe the Nathan he uses before the recurring Zuckerman as his fictional self (and therefore his other other) is meant to pay homage to Hawthorne, Hale, or Bumppo? That's my father's name you're talking about. Nathan Smith. Look it up in Yahoo or Google or on the Ellis Island guest list, if you dare. Or else you can just go on dreaming your Let's Pretend dreams.

The struggle, as I see it, have always seen ir, is between his efforts to turn me into fiction, and mine, to maintain myself as fact. The fantasy-reality motif is further weighted toward fantasy when Roth begins to ask himself whether this Kahane-Pipik plot he has made a commitment to thwart exists outside of his imagination, leaving me to wonder how far I have wandered from reality myself (although on the surface I know it's Pipik he's dealing with here, not me).

Upon leaving the Demjanjuk trial, where he is relieved to find no sign of a plot, Roth comes upon a loud exchange going on in the street between a Jewish Paul Bunyan and a plumpish priest distributing pamphlets commemorating the presence of Christianity in the Ukraine for a millennium (which might be seen as a showdown between Moishe and Pipik, written word and spoken word, Gentile and Jew); with the giant shouting out the names of Ukrainians—Chmielnicki, Bandera, Petlura—who had led pogroms against the Jews.

In and of itself, despite Roth's attempts to connect it to the Demjanjuk plot, the scene seems to provide yet another diversion from the object of Roth's disdain—yours truly and truthfully—until I recall a scene from my second book, where the bitter Jesuit-like Hebrew school teacher terrifies his students with graphic descriptions of pogroms through the ages.

> 'Do you have any idea what it means, the word *pogrom*? Have you maybe heard your parents talk about it in the next room? Let me hear your wisdom, men and women of tomorrow. Have your arms fallen off from your bodies, or do you know nothing? Well, it's the murder of a whole people, and if they had their way, none of us would be alive today. But killing wasn't enough for Chmielnicki and his bandits. They burned us at the stake, tore our flesh with pliers, cut off our ears and thumbs, plucked out our eyes, hammered nails into our skulls, ripped open the bodies of our women, then sewed them up again with live animals inside.'[3]

Mar Eisen (or Mr. Iron) was one of two teachers in the small neighborhood Hebrew school I attended after public school. He wore fedora hats rather than yarmulkes, the brim pulled down over his thick glasses, and he never smiled. In fact, his mouth always looked as if he were about to spit. We all knew that if we misbehaved we would be sent to his class as punishment.

There's no longer any doubt in my mind why Roth has chosen to display this street exchange here, near the end of the book. What he's doing, in effect and effectively, is turning my scene of terror as seen through the eyes of a sensitive child into one of comic relief (or ridicule) before bidding me a final adieu. At the same time, of course, he makes sure to measure my unpublished second book

---

[3]Smith, Martin, *Flowers for the Dead*, 1968, p. 108.

against his published twentieth, with my hateful tyrant of a teacher looking on.

An even more compelling reason for this scene then comes to mind, as Roth's red-headed seven-foot Jew with immense chin and hands conjures up a photograph by Diane Arbus entitled 'A Jewish giant at home with his parents in the Bronx, N.Y. 1970,' someone with whom, by the way, I once shot baskets at a small upstate camp-hotel. I had just finished serving dinner in the main dining room, and liked to loosen up after a meal by practicing foul shots on the basketball court, since most of the waiters played for desserts just about every day. It hadn't turned dark yet, but the courts were empty.

An imposing figure, he sauntered down the low hill toward me to watch, and I threw him the ball. The few times I had seen him he was off by himself, and I couldn't help but imagine how lonely he must have felt. I remember he shot his foul shots underhanded (which was no longer the popular style). The ball looked like a softball in his massive hands. His long arms were stiff like the parts of a machine, and his voice was as deep as the bottom of the sea. I saw him again one night, years later, looming up out of the subway station at 181st Street I was about to enter. I hesitated, thought of speaking to him (not that I knew him well), but decided not to (whether out of shyness or intimidation, I'll never know), and have regretted it ever since.

After skirting around this incident, Roth finally gets to the point vis-à-vis *moi* and *moi* shadow and makes it without any equivocation whatsoever. That there was no way for Pipik and him to coexist, no way to separate his thoughts from those of the other and maybe therefore from mine. Now I ask you, is this supposed to be Roth speaking for me or sending a not-so-subtle message to me? If he's speaking for himself, and why wouldn't he be, he seems to be calling for the end of our coexistence and therefore my demise rather than his quiet withdrawal from my life. What I'm trying to figure out, though, is how he intends to carry out this metamorphosis without my cooperation.

Then perhaps for the first time he reveals the extent of my effect on him, although not its cause or origins, when he accuses me of somehow dwarfing his significance and the extent of his potential. So once again, for whatever reason, he feels compelled to express my sentiments about him as if they were his, while chiding my loss of freedom as an after-thought; but maybe they're his sentiments as well, which leaves us with no room for reconciliation.

I mean, what the hell is this guy's problem anyway? Has he mistaken me for someone else named Smith he knew years ago, a hateful Smitty of his unhappy school days, or a colleague in melancholy clothing? Or does he believe I'm someone who changed my name under cover of darkness into a placebo cough drop? If these were prehistoric times, we'd no doubt be having it out in a final duel with the jaw bones of asses; but because we are civilized, middle-aged, and sedentary beings sitting on our asses most of the time, we do our fighting over cell phones and e-mails and sometimes through the pages of best-selling novels and letters to the editor, as Roth seems intent on drawing me into mental if not mortal combat of one kind or another, although I'm still trying to figure out why and how.

Like the double Humbert, words are all I have to play with. Roth too, I assume, although he seems more inclined to play with mine. If you keep riding the words, though, they will eventually take you to places you may not want to visit. In the past I might have picked up a pen, found a blank sheet of paper, and written the history of the world in twenty-five words or less, but not anymore. I am too wary of big brother Roth hovering over my shoulder like an enemy aircraft to do anything about it. Whenever I do finish a work, though, and take it around town, I am usually told it's been done by Philip Roth. I'm sure if I started writing poetry, he would become the poet laureate of the United States.

Whatever you may believe, I am not an escaped character from one of Roth's novels, despite his efforts to get me there. Real life is the novel I've inhabited from as far back as I can remember, and my only purpose, not unlike Roth's, is to have you read these pages of mine, while I avoid being inserted into his. Not an easy juggling act, I assure you, but let the chips (with their software pretensions) fall where they may.

Meanwhile, reverting back to his usual methods, Roth, despite open window and locked door, presents himself as having been taken prisoner in an empty classroom by forces unknown, just as I am on the verge of announcing my own captivity, by forces known, within the indomitable walls of Roth's book. If his double is not here anymore, as I suspect, and I am not his double, then where is he, and where am I?

Despite his denials, I find myself being moved by him toward the end of something. As reader, where do you stand? On the outskirts of thought or the instincts of interpretation, while Roth waxes poetic, or believes he does, on Negev sands? Well, let me remind you that the creative process doesn't end with the writing of the book, but the reading of it, as I hope you are now doing.

Left alone in the room, with his fear continuing to mount, Roth tries to make sense of the predicament he finds himself in. As he focuses on the plot he first sought to escape in the morning, it is not clear, as on earlier occasions (since plots are so much a part of the book), which plot he has in mind, the one to kidnap Demjanjuk, the younger, or the one that governs the direction of his (or, as he sees it, Pipik's) book. In the end he considers it his only way out (plots usually are), but first he feels compelled to critique it as not ringing true, lacking depth and structure, and being without design or direction. Yet as bad as he makes it seem, he would prefer to return to the role, no matter how ridiculous, he has been playing in it.

> Roth seems to have reduced our so-called showdown to a battle of the books, his and mine, with him supposedly wanting to remain a character in mine (although I don't believe a word of it), while I am willing to do almost anything to avoid finding myself in his. Of course, before it's all over he has to put my book down one more time, using (as you might expect) many of the criticisms I have made or thought about his work. As for mine, I dare you to point out one single instance where I have attempted to deceive the reader or resorted to treachery in telling my story. Roth is merely turning our books inside out, substituting his for mine.[4]

So what does he do next? He calls out to Pipik, wants to know if he's out there, if he is the architect of this absurd plot, meaning, this time, the one that has resulted in his having been taken prisoner. He would like an answer, demands one in fact, and maintains that he was never antagonistic toward Pipik. He calls for a careful looking backward, pleads for an in-depth search of what has gone on between them. Seems to be on the verge of apologizing and asking forgiveness, when he reverts back to his old role as the injured party, asks if Pipik is without blame.

> Of course not, nor have I claimed to be. You're the one who's created the facsimile, the *doublesse oblige*. I'm here. Are you there? This does not come out of my imagination, but is my response, as I stated in the very beginning, to what you've written about me over the years. This book (my book) is an effort to offer my remembrance of things

---

[4]Smith, Martin, ***Goodbye, Philip Roth***, Pleasure Boat Studio, 2011, p. 78.

> past, not yours or Proust's. You may claim whatever you want, but try as you might, you cannot prove that you have been provoked by me nearly as much as I have by you.[5]

Without so much as an extended pause between thoughts, Roth is back in his confessional mode. Admitting that he may have been overly confrontational in the past, he is now prepared to make a serious effort to learn how to be more understanding of Pipik before going off half-cocked. This is no lie, he declares. Yet he realizes that Pipik, now in control, would treat him with contempt if he started brown-nosing him (as Pipik, ironically, had done to him when they first met). He seems to be playing the good cop-bad cop gambit, so to speak, while being the only cop in the building.

> So there you are, on your knees as if in prayer, hands up, white flag in one of them, playing the victim again, so your faithful readers will sympathize with your plight and hold me, a fellow reader, in contempt; when I'm the one at wit's end, the target of your sarcastic barbs. Why don't you listen to your own words for a change. It's not merely your plaintive resolution that you will make a greater effort to empathize with me without revealing how you intend to do so that I question, but the more hostile use of firing-squad imagery to make your point, when you, in fact, are the one holding the gun in your hand, the knife at my throat. Is this your way of apologizing to me? Who are you kidding, Roth? Trying to learn? About me? You trying to forget me would be more to my liking.[6]

---

[5]Ibid., pp. 78–9.
[6]Ibid., pp. 79–80.

But in the ensuing silence, without even the hint of a response to his plea, Roth begins to lose control of himself. In a lengthy apostrophe to Pipik, his voice quavering with emotion, he begs for forgiveness, or, if not that, at least for some omen or indication that will let him know Pipik is out there listening to him, and that he, Roth, is not alone.

> I am under the auspices of free will, free plunge into whirlpool bath, toward whipsaw landing, wanting to right myself, write myself, by writing a tale of two writers, while climbing rungs of words to what I believe is a logical Tower of Babel, with everyone babbling in my ears. My father having died too early for such dementia to occur makes me wonder if I am headed in that direction, with my mother having already made the trip before me.[7]

At this point in his one-sided dialogue with himself, Roth seems to achieve yet another epiphany with regard to Pipik. After acknowledging his initial awkwardness in their early encounters, his misreading of Pipik's commitment to being Roth's double, he realizes that the only way to make amends is to sincerely address Pipik as Philip Roth, accept him as his true double, thereby allowing Pipik to appear and the two of them to put an end to their differences.

> Playing word games like Ping Pong and sing song leads to too many words, too many meanings. Why do we need so many words to say the same things over and over again. I mean, I exist outside of Roth, over here, the guy writing this damn book that you'll probably never read anyway. Or do I? Does anyone exist outside of anyone? These words, I

---

[7]Ibid., p. 80.

> believe, are still mine. They are being used to describe the name of another rose. Or is it the same rose? Whether the name is Pipik or Philip Roth or Martin Smith makes no difference, for in the end they're only names.[8]

Roth calls out his first name as if he were talking to himself, and perhaps he is. There is no method to the madness. There never is. Nor is there an answer. He calls out again and again, without receiving any response. Is he expecting one from himself? He keeps on babbling about not being Pipik's enemy, when no one ever said he was, except maybe himself. He is upset by how things have ended up between them. Now he wants to be Pipik's friend. Yet it's his fear that drives him. But there is nada, nothing, no reply, just the endless space and the ensuing silence, and if Pipik is there, he's not saying a word.

> In spite of all my efforts, the worms have entered the cool tombs. I know they are there, although they take their time as usual. I am the inert form they will feed on when they're good and ready, my nostrils the tunnels they will crawl through to get to the other side. There is no need for them to hurry, since I am already reconciled to being served up as their ritual meal, where the winds blow and the leaves sway and the worst of days leads to the worst of nights, and rising from one's ashes isn't as easy as it's made out to be.[9]

As a last resort, Roth flagellates himself with faint criticism. He admits, by how he addressed Pipik in the past, to have put himself

---

[8]Ibid., pp. 80–1.
[9]Ibid., p. 81.

on a pedestal while lowering Pipik on the ladder of esteem. And now, based purely on fear, he wants their relationship to be on a first-name basis, and that name to be Philip Roth, a name shared by both of them; but if Pipik is there, he isn't answering. The chances are, though, that he isn't there, that no one's there.

MARTIN SMITH is a novelist, screenwriter, and teacher. His credits include *Flora's Dream* and *Under the Rainbow*. He lives in New York City with his wife and is at work on another book.

A Path to the Sea ~ Liliana Ursu, trans. from Romanian by Tess Gallagher and Adam Sorkin ~ poems ~ $15.95

Toys in My Attic ~ Russell Connor ~ humor ~ $13.95

Beautiful Passing Lives ~ Ed Harkness ~ poems ~ $15

Immortality ~ Mike O'Connor ~ poems ~ $16

Painting Brooklyn ~ Paintings by Nina Talbot, Poetry by Esther Cohen ~ $20

Ghost Farm ~ Pamela Stewart ~ poems ~ $13

Unknown Places ~ Peter Kantor, trans. from Hungarian by Michael Blumenthal ~ poems ~ $14

Leaving Yesler ~ Peter Bacho ~ fiction ~ $16

Moonlight in the Redemptive Forest ~ Michael Daley ~ poems (includes a CD) ~ $16

Jew's Harp ~ Walter Hess ~ poems ~ $14

The Light on Our Faces ~ Lee Whitman-Raymond ~ poems ~ $13

Crossing the Water: The Hawaii-Alaska Trilogies ~ Irving Warner ~ fiction ~ $16

Unnecessary Talking: The Montesano Stories ~ Mike O'Connor ~ fiction ~ $16

God Is a Tree, and Other Middle-Age Prayers ~ Esther Cohen ~ poems ~ $10

Home & Away: The Old Town Poems ~ Kevin Miller ~ $15

The Woman Who Wrote "King Lear," And Other Stories ~ Louis Phillips ~ $16

Weinstock Among the Dying ~ Michael Blumenthal ~ fiction ~ $18

The War Journal of Lila Ann Smith ~ Irving Warner ~ historical fiction ~ $18

Dream of the Dragon Pool: A Daoist Quest ~ Albert A. Dalia ~ fantasy ~ $18

Monique ~ Luisa Coehlo, trans. from Portuguese by Maria do Carmo de Vasconcelos and Dolores DeLuise ~ fiction ~ $14

Against Romance ~ Michael Blumenthal ~ poetry ~ $14

Artrage ~ Everett Aison ~ fiction ~ $15

Days We Would Rather Know ~ Michael Blumenthal ~ poems ~ $14

Puget Sound: 15 Stories ~ C. C. Long ~ fiction ~ $14

Homicide My Own ~ Anne Argula ~ fiction (mystery) ~ $16

Craving Water ~ Mary Lou Sanelli ~ poems ~ $15

When the Tiger Weeps ~ Mike O'Connor ~ poetry and prose ~ 15

Wagner, Descending: The Wrath of the Salmon Queen ~ Irving Warner ~ fiction ~ $16

Concentricity ~ Sheila E. Murphy ~ poems ~ $13.95

Schilling, from a study in lost time ~ Terrell Guillory ~ fiction ~ $17

Rumours: A Memoir of a British POW in WWII ~ Chas Mayhead ~ nonfiction ~ $16

The Immigrant's Table ~ Mary Lou Sanelli ~ poems and recipes ~ $14

The Enduring Vision of Norman Mailer ~ Dr. Barry H. Leeds ~ criticism ~ $18

Women in the Garden ~ Mary Lou Sanelli ~ poems ~ $14

Pronoun Music ~ Richard Cohen ~ short stories ~ $16

If You Were With Me Everything Would Be All Right ~ Ken Harvey ~ short stories ~ $16

The 8th Day of the Week ~ Al Kessler ~ fiction ~ $16

Another Life, and Other Stories ~ Edwin Weihe short stories ~ $16

Saying the Necessary ~ Edward Harkness ~ poems ~ $14

Nature Lovers ~ Charles Potts ~ poems ~ $10

In Memory of Hawks, & Other Stories from Alaska ~ Irving Warner ~ fiction ~ $15

The Politics of My Heart ~ William Slaughter ~ poems ~ $13

The Rape Poems ~ Frances Driscoll ~ poems ~ $13

When History Enters the House: Essays from Central Europe ~ Michael Blumenthal ~ $15

Setting Out: The Education of Lili ~ Tung Nien ~ trans. fm Chinese by Mike O'Connor ~ fiction ~ $15

Our Chapbook Series:

No. 1: ***The Handful of Seeds: Three and a Half Essays*** ~ Andrew Schelling ~ $7 ~ nonfiction

No. 2: ***Original Sin*** ~ Michael Daley ~ $8 ~ poetry

No. 3: ***Too Small to Hold You*** ~ Kate Reavey ~ $8 ~ poetry

No. 4: ***The Light on Our Faces***— re-issued in non-chapbook (see above list)

No. 5: ***Eye*** ~ William Bridges ~ $8 ~ poetry

No. 6: ***Selected New Poems of Rainer Maria Rilke*** ~ trans. fm German by Alice Derry ~ $10 ~ poetry

No. 7: ***Through High Still Air: A Season at Sourdough Mountain*** ~ Tim McNulty ~ $9 ~ poetry, prose

No. 8: ***Sight Progress*** ~ Zhang Er, trans. fm Chinese by Rachel Levitsky ~ $9 ~ prosepoems

No. 9: ***The Perfect Hour*** ~ Blas Falconer ~ $9 ~ poetry

No. 10: ***Fervor*** ~ Zaedryn Meade ~ $10 ~ poetry

No. 11: ***Some Ducks*** ~ Tim McNulty ~ $10 ~ poetry

No. 12: ***Late August*** ~ Barbara Brackney ~ $10 ~ poetry

No. 13: ***The Right to Live Poetically*** ~ Emily Haines ~ $9 ~ poetry

Orders:

Pleasure Boat Studio books are available by order from your bookstore, directly from our website, or through the following:

SPD (Small Press Distribution)
Tel. 800-869-7553, Fax 510-524-0852

Partners/West Tel. 425-227-8486,
Fax 425-204-2448

Baker & Taylor Tel. 800-775-1100,
Fax 800-775-7480

Ingram Tel. 615-793-5000,
Fax 615-287-5429

Amazon.com or **Barnesandnoble.com**

Pleasure Boat Studio: A Literary Press
201 West 89th Street
New York, NY 10024
Tel. / Fax: 888-810-5308
www.pleasureboatstudio.com / pleasboat@nyc.rr.com